GOING DOWN SWINGING

Skye Fargo had been trying to get his hands on Pony-Runs-Long for a long time. The trouble was, now the Cheyenne war chief had his hands on Skye.

Those huge hands were around the Trailsman's throat. Desperately Fargo slammed his right fist against one side of the war chief's head and his left fist against the other side. Then Fargo powered a right to the man's solar plexus. The war chief just grunted and tightened his grip.

Fargo's senses began fading. And through the fog filling his brain, Skye heard the Indian's triumphant snarl, "Die!"

Skye Fargo was down to his last breath—and he was clean out of tricks. . . .

BLAZING NEW TRAILS
WITH SKYE FARGO

☐ **THE TRAILSMAN #107: GUNSMOKE GULCH by Jon Sharpe.** Skye Fargo blasts a white-slaving ring apart and discovers that a beauty named Annie has a clue to a gold mine worth slaving for—a proposition that makes Skye ready to blaze a trail through a gunsmoke screen of lethal lies. (168038—$3.50)

☐ **THE TRAILSMAN #109: LONE STAR LIGHTNING by Jon Sharpe.** Skye Fargo on a Texas manhunt with two deadly weapons—a blazing gun and a fiery female. (168801—$3.50)

☐ **THE TRAILSMAN #110: COUNTERFEIT CARGO by Jon Sharpe.** The pay was too good for Skye Fargo to turn down, so he's guiding a wagon train loaded with evil and heading for hell. (168941—$3.50)

☐ **THE TRAILSMAN #111: BLOOD CANYON by Jon Sharpe.** Kills Fast, the savage Cheyenne medicine man, hated Skye Fargo like poison. And when Skye followed a perverse pair of paleskin fugitives into redskin hands, Kills Fast wasn't about to live up to his name. (169204—$3.50)

☐ **THE TRAILSMAN #112: THE DOOMSDAY WAGONS by Jon Sharpe.** Skye Fargo follows a trail of corpses on a trip through hell for a showdown with marauding redskins. (169425—$3.50)

☐ **THE TRAILSMAN #113: SOUTHERN BELLES by Jon Sharpe.** The Trailsman had plenty of bullets in his gunbelt when a Mississippi paddle-wheeler found itself in a mist of mystery as ripe young beauties were plucked from its cabins. (169635—$3.50)

THE TRAILSMAN

113

SOUTHERN BELLES

by

Jon Sharpe

A SIGNET BOOK

SIGNET
Published by the Penguin Group
Penguin Books USA Inc., 375 Hudson Street,
New York, New York 10014, U.S.A.
Penguin Books Ltd, 27 Wrights Lane,
London W8 5TZ, England
Penguin Books Australia Ltd, Ringwood,
Victoria, Australia
Penguin Books Canada Ltd, 2801 John Street,
Markham, Ontario, Canada L3R 1B4
Penguin Books (N.Z.) Ltd, 182-190 Wairau Road,
Auckland 10, New Zealand

Penguin Books Ltd, Registered Offices:
Harmondsworth, Middlesex, England

First published by Signet, an imprint of New American Library,
a division of Penguin Books USA Inc.

First Printing, May, 1991

10 9 8 7 6 5 4 3 2 1

The first chapter of this book previously appeared in *The Doomsday Wagons*,
the one hundred twelfth volume in this series.

REGISTERED TRADEMARK—MARCA REGISTRADA

Printed in the United States of America

PUBLISHER'S NOTE
This is a work of fiction. Names, characters, places, and incidents either
are the product of the author's imagination or are used fictitiously, and any
resemblance to actual persons, living or dead, events, or locales is entirely
coincidental.

The Trailsman

Beginnings . . . they bend the tree and they mark the man. Skye Fargo was born when he was eighteen. Terror was his midwife, vengeance his first cry. Killing spawned Skye Fargo, ruthless, cold-blooded murder. Out of the acrid smoke of gunpowder still hanging in the air, he rose, cried out a promise never forgotten.

The Trailsman they began to call him all across the West: searcher, scout, hunter, the man who could see where others only looked, his skills for hire but not his soul, the man who lived each day to the fullest, yet trailed each tomorrow. Skye Fargo, the Trailsman, the seeker who could take the wildness of a land and the wanting of a woman and make them his own.

Summer, 1860, on the Mississippi River, whose muddy waters conceal dark deeds and shady schemes, and where death lurks just below the surface . . .

1

The big man astride the magnificent black-and-white pinto stallion followed the west bank of a canyon stream in Montana Territory, deep inside Sioux country. Although aware that friction existed between the Indians and bluecoats at Fort Laramie, far to the south, he rode easy in the saddle; the Sioux were his friends, the troopers as white of skin as he.

General Scott McRae, a man he'd never met, had dispatched twenty-five troopers with orders to punish the seven bands of Lakota Sioux roaming west of the Black Hills. General McRae was convinced one of the bands had attacked a wagon train of settlers and massacred them all. The remains of the wagons and settlers had been found within Lakota territory, ill-defined as it was.

The survivors of a Two Kettle *tiospaye* had told the Trailsman all of this information two days ago. They also mentioned being shelled by a big gun—the "iron giant on wheels," one had called the cannon.

"The bluecoats struck without warning early in the morning," the wounded warrior told Fargo. "Our women were building cooking fires outside the tepees when the iron giant roared. The ground beneath my belly bounced and shook. The women screamed. They ran inside their tepees to hide. Then the bluecoats attacked us. They shot many people, Trailsman—women, children, and old, helpless elders. Some butchered us with their long knives while others burned our tepees. The ten of us you see played like we were dead. Between us we know enough of the white man's words to piece together what their leader said to his soldiers. This General McRae does a bad thing. We Lakota didn't bother those wagons. Neither did we kill any of the *wasicun*. War Chief Pony-Runs-Long did it. I speak the truth, Trailsman."

Skye Fargo knew the Cheyenne war chief. Pony-Runs-Long was insane and reckless, but bold at best. He had vowed never to make peace with the Great Father in Washington. For years the cavalry had been chasing him and his warriors, but the cunning war chief gave them the slip every time the troopers got close. Now it appeared Pony-Runs-Long had done it again, and had shifted the blame onto the Lakota, his natural enemy.

Fargo moved up the canyon slowly, scanning through the green canopy of whispering pine, cottonwood, and weeping willow at the jagged, windblown crests of the sheer, rocky walls on either side of him. He paused when he rode into a clear spot and took a closer look. He knew Sans Arc were in the canyon. Maybe warriors on the ridges would see him. If any were up there, they didn't reveal their presence to him. Fargo rode on.

He'd gone less than a hundred yards when muted echoes of cannon and rifle fire reverberated off the canyon walls. The sounds came from far up the canyon. Fargo nudged the Ovaro into a gallop. There was no need for a faster pace; the detachment of soldiers would finish their work and be gone by the time he got there.

Rounding a bend, he smelled smoke. Riding farther, he saw wisps of smoke hanging low over the stream and among lower branches of trees. All the gunfire had ceased. In the far distance he heard women wailing, and he quickened the powerful stallion's gait. The smoke became increasingly pronounced the closer he got to the encampment. Then he saw it, or what was left of it.

The encampment stood in the opening among the pine trees over on the east bank near the mouth of the canyon. Beyond that opening stretched a prairie where buffalo herds—the Lakota people's main source of food—roamed, grazing at leisure. On that prairie rode the column of troopers, mere specks now. The iron giant rolled at the rear of the column.

Fargo reined the Ovaro toward the burning tepees. None had their covering intact. The buffalo hides so carefully tanned by the women—it took a minimum of twelve—and painstakingly sewn together with threads of sinew, lay smoldering on the ground around the tepee poles. Several tepees had been demolished in an instant by cannon balls. The people's meager possessions were scattered everywhere: colorful shields, most with eagle feathers attached; water bags made from buffalo stomachs; gourd dippers; cradle boards, several with hoods that still smoldered; and buffalo robes by the dozens. Black Cheyenne or Crow scalps fluttered in the updraft of tepee poles still standing and aflame.

Half-naked warriors lay where they had been gunned down or met death by a flashing saber. Crumpled bodies of women—some still carrying their babies—lay where they were caught while fleeing the soldiers. A baby with a bleeding head wound sat crying between its mother's outstretched, lifeless arms. An old man stood on wobbly legs, watching the tepee poles burn. He seemed confused by it all, as though he couldn't believe what had happened, as though he could blink and make it be as before.

Four wounded warriors staggered to the old man as Fargo rode up and reined the pinto to a halt. He dismounted and went to the crying infant first. Blood from a gash in the naked girl's forehead streamed over her eyes and down her face. Fargo believed she would survive, albeit with an ugly scar that in later life she could point to and tell the little ones gathered around her about the day the bluecoats came. He removed his neckerchief and wiped the blood from the little girl's eyes and face, then tied the neckerchief around her head to stop the flow of blood. He hefted her in his arms and carried her to the warriors and old man.

Handing the child to the warrior least wounded—like the old man, the brave was in shock more than anything else, although he bled from a saber wound on his left thigh—Fargo turned his attention to the warrior's companions. All three had multiple rifle or pistol wounds, one so bad that Fargo couldn't imagine what was holding the man together. Speaking in the Lakota dialect, Fargo told the dazed warriors, "Sit and let me have a look at your wounds."

The warrior shook his head, then fell dead, leaking blood from six holes in his body.

Fargo moved to the next man. He had been shot in the right shoulder and creased by a bullet on the left upper arm. The bullet that hit his shoulder had gone clear through. The young warrior appeared healthy enough to make Fargo reckon the man would live. The warrior had scars above both nipples, attesting that he was a sundancer. As such, the crease on his arm meant nothing. Fargo told him, "Find some fresh sage. Strip off the tender leaves and roll them into two balls, then pack one where the bullet went in, the other where it came out."

The warrior nodded and walked away.

As Fargo stepped to the next man, six warriors rode in from the mouth of the canyon. Sliding off their ponies, they looked questioningly at the big white man, as though he were responsible for the death and destruction they saw. It was a tense moment when the big man withdrew his Colt and handed it to one of them to show he had come in peace.

The warrior promptly returned the weapon to him and grunted, "We saw bluecoats riding away on the prairie. We know you couldn't do this alone. But you could have helped the bluecoats. Why are you here, *wasicun*? To make sure all our relatives died?"

Before Fargo could answer, the old man muttered dryly, "Be quiet, Chases Bears, before your tongue shames you. The white man came after the bluecoats

12

killed everybody. He had nothing to do with what your eyes see. Now, Trailsman, you can speak. Tell us why you are here."

Fargo proceeded to wipe blood from the back left-shoulder gunshot wound of the warrior he had stepped to. The slug had ripped open a long gash on the warrior's back, but not penetrated his body. The warrior was in no danger of an early death. Fargo answered, "I came to warn my Sans Arc brothers and sisters that the cavalry was looking for them, to hurt them, for something bad the Cheyenne did."

"Unh," the old man grunted. He swept a hand in a wide, flat arc and went on, "Then the Cheyenne, they are the cause of all this?"

"Yes," Fargo began. "Pony-Runs-Long attacked a wagon train in Wyoming Territory. All settlers were massacred. Bluecoats from Fort Laramie found them. Because it happened in Lakota hunting territory they—"

Chases Bears interrupted. He spat angrily, then spoke. "Enough. We know Pony-Runs-Long. He has been causing trouble for me and my brothers a long time." Turning to the old man, Chases Bears said tenderly, "Sit in shade, Tunkasila Two Eagles. We will take care of everything."

"No," the grandfather replied. "It is my duty to help. There are many people to be buried. Raise a big scaffold. We will send them to the spirit world in the Lakota way. Find my pipe."

Chases Bears and the other five nonwounded warriors walked away to obey Grandfather Two Eagles. Fargo tended to the third warrior's wounds, two pistol shots, both in his lower neck, both fired at extremely close range. Both bullets had missed arteries, the only reason the warrior still lived. The weakened man was in no condition to help the burial party. Fargo suggested he too pack his wounds with sage, then sit in the shade.

Though the warrior complied with Fargo's first suggestion, he did not accept the second. He helped his brothers build the scaffold. Fargo did, too. Two Eagles oversaw its construction at the site he selected on top of the east wall of the canyon, where it dropped off and met the prairie.

In Fargo's opinion it was truly a remarkable feat. Not only was it required of them to fell the many lodgepole pine to support the huge scaffold, then lug them up to the crest and construct the lattice-shaped platform on which the dead would be laid to rest, they also had to carry the dead up to the scaffold. Not a small chore for seven able-bodied men and three walking-wounded.

As the dead were brought to the scaffold, the three women cut a bit of hair from each or snipped off fingernails or toenails. Fargo watched them put the trimmings on a large piece of buckskin spread on the ground under the platform. The pile of hair and nail clippings grew larger and larger. He knew that after the burial ceremony the buckskin and cuttings would be tied into a bundle and kept in a secret place for one year, at which time the bundle would be buried, thereby releasing the souls of the dead. In the meantime a similar bundle would be prepared. It would be hidden, too, but not as secretly as the first bundle. There were those—such as the Cheyenne and Crow— who would dearly love to find the bundle, open it, and scatter the trimmings in the four winds, thus releasing the souls prematurely and causing them to wander forever and not enter the spirit world. It was serious business. Fargo respected it.

Fargo counted thirty-two bodies as they were passed up to him and Chases Bears to arrange on the platform. A full moon hung high in the starlit sky before they put the last lifeless form on the platform.

They dropped to the ground and joined the others already sitting in a circle around a small fire. Fargo watched Two Eagles fill two halves of semilarge geodes with a mixture of flat cedar, sweetgrass, and crumbled sage, the Sioux's sacred incense ingredients, then drop a small, glowing ember into each. The old man took one of the smoldering geodes under the scaffold platform and held it high as he walked back and forth beneath the bodies. In this way all were purified by the smoke from the incense. Finished, he set the geode on the ground beneath the platform and left it there to smolder out.

Then he brought the other geode with him when he returned to the circle of men and women, who sat facing a small fire in its center. Between his position on the eastern rim of the circle lay the open buckskin of trimmings and his pipe bag, both resting on a east-to-west axis cutting through his position and the fire. The buckskin was nearest to the fire, the pipe bag within easy reach when he sat.

Two Eagles held the smoldering geode close to the buckskin and "washed" it and the trimmings thoroughly with the incense smoke. Finally he set the geode on the ground in front of his pipe bag, stepped to his position in the circle, and sat on his haunches, facing the fire.

Fargo, the warriors, and the women sat and remained silent as Two Eagles began the sacred rite, Releasing of the Soul. The old man rubbed sage on both his palms, then handed the sage to the warrior sitting to his left, who did the same, then passed it to the warrior sitting on his left. The ball of sage moved sunwise around the circle so that each person could purify his hands before receiving the sacred pipe.

The pipe bag before Two Eagles was liberally adorned with porcupine quills, tiny beads of all colors, and the opening tied with a length of thong fashioned out of buckskin. Secured to the thong was his *cungleska*, a small medicine wheel backed by a hard-to-come-by, hence treasured, piece of shiny seashell shaped to conform with the circular medicine wheel. Tied to the sacred hoop were the two eagle tail feathers Two Eagles had received during his naming ceremony. They were misshapen now, the tips curled, some of the individual feathers constituting the whole missing altogether.

Fargo knew the old man revered the *cungleska* and feathers; they were the old man's bond that connected him to the past, present, and future.

Slowly, reverently, Two Eagles removed the *cungleska* and feathers, then opened the pipe bag. He took out the bowl and long stem of his pipe. He moved parts back and forth in the smoke rising from the geode to purify each. Fargo watched him firmly but gently connect the bowl and stem, then pass the whole pipe through the smoke. Then the old man opened his tobacco pouch, removed a pinch of the sacred *cincasa*, and offered it to the spirit in the west.

The warriors and Fargo began singing the pipe-filling song, which continued while the old man made similar offerings to the spirits in the north, east, south, to his Maka Ina, Mother Earth, which he held to the ground, to Wanka Tanka, the Great Spirit, which he held skyward. The seventh pinch was for the spotted eagle who would carry his and their later prayers aloft and release them into the universe.

The old man stood, faced west, pointed the pipe's stem in that direction, and offered the first of six prayers, which he repeated as he faced the spirits in the other three directions; he looked down when he prayed to Mother Earth and up when he invoked the Great Spirit. "O Wanka Tanka, Two Eagles is praying to you. Hear me, Wanka Tanka. I am praying for you to take the souls of my dead relatives across the great waters, there to be among their ancestors, who live in peace with all human beings' souls, even the *Wasicun*'s. O Wanka Tanka forgive the bluecoats for what they did this day, for they know not the truth. In your own way punish those who are responsible. They are crazy, Wanka Tanka, and must be stopped from causing trouble. *Me-tock-we-ah-see*." Having said the Lakota equivalent of amen, Two Eagles sat and lit his pipe with the burning end of a twig taken from the fire.

After taking a few draws and exhaling the smoke, he started the pipe around the circle. When it came back to him, he smoked it out, disassembled the two parts, and returned them to the pipe bag. He said, "*Me-tock-we-ah-see*." The ceremony was over.

The women wrapped and tied the buckskin bundle. Fargo and the warriors followed Two Eagles down to the destroyed *tiospaye*.

When they got there, Chases Bears turned to face Fargo and asked, "Where will you go?"

"I'm looking for a white woman. She was taken from a wagon train passing through or near your lands. All I know is she was taken by Indians. Which tribe or band is unknown."

One of the other warriors spoke up. "Chases Bears, I know of such a white woman."

"Then, tell us, Crying Fox," Chases Bears insisted.

"By all means, do," Fargo added.

"The Miniconju have her," Crying Fox began. "They captured her during a night raid to steal Cheyenne women from Pony-Runs-Long's camp. Hoksila told me they were surprised to see a white face among the Cheyenne faces when they got back to their encampment."

"She's well, I hope?" Fargo inquired. "Did you see her? Describe her to me."

"No, I didn't see her. Hoksila's hunting party and the one I was in met on the prairie one morning. He told me about the raid and stealing the white woman by mistake."

"How long ago was that?" Fargo pressed.

"During the new moon before the last full moon. Raids to steal women and ponies always happen when the night sky is good and dark."

About thirty-eight or so days ago, Fargo thought. "When did your hunting party bump into Hoksila's?" Fargo asked.

"Ten moons ago," Crying Fox replied.

"Did Hoksila mention what the Miniconju did with her?"

"Hoksila said none of the warriors wanted her. He

17

said they gave her to an old Miniconju woman who could no longer gather wood."

"Crying Fox, will you take me to Hoksila?"

"For what you have done this day, yes, I will take you to my brothers the Miniconju."

The three women walked up carrying two identical bundles. Fargo noticed one bundle had been double-tied. He didn't know whether it or the other one held the souls of the dead Sans Arcs. Nobody other than the three women would ever know, and they would die before revealing the truth. All three women had shorn their hair. Though they looked funny, Fargo didn't so much as grin. They were in mourning for one full year. Two of them had also cut off the tips of their noses, a sure sign that they were now widows. They made themselves ugly on purpose, so no man would have them, so all who saw them would know they were grieving widows. It was the custom, a show of respect for their departed husbands.

The young woman having a whole nose took the baby girl from the wounded warrior.

Fargo said, "Well, Crying Fox, there is nothing more for us to do here. If we ride hard and fast maybe we will find your Miniconju brothers before the army does."

They shook hands all around, then Fargo and Crying Fox mounted up. The warriors, women, and old man watched them ride out of the canyon and disappear on the grassy prairie.

Fargo headed north, into the great unknown.

2

At twilight on the morning of the second day the Trailsman and the Sans Arc warrior spotted the Miniconju *tiospaye*. So did the detachment from Fort Laramie . . . and a sizable force of Cheyenne. Fargo reined the Ovaro to a halt. He sat easy in the saddle while he and Crying Fox studied the situation.

The encampment of fourteen tepees surrounded a large pool fed by a narrow, gurgling creek. Cottonwood and pine competed for water in the creek and pool, forming a tunnel-shaped canopy on either side of the pool, where the creek flowed in and out. The Miniconju's corral of ropes tied to trees stood a stone's throw away upstream. Fargo and his companion stood side by side at a spot where they had a clear view of the opposing forces.

The troops were in a slight depression less than a half-mile away from the *tiospaye* and due west of it. Soldiers were bringing the cannon into firing position. The other troopers were mounted up and in a long line ready to charge.

Crying Fox watched the Cheyenne riding slowly, coming toward the encampment, hidden from view to the camp and the troopers by dense, low-growing foliage in the east. Fargo believed neither they nor the army were aware of the other's presence. And the unsuspecting Miniconju were totally unaware of the presence of either. Several women hovered near outside cooking fires. Their babies lay in cradle boards propped on logs so the infants could see their mothers and be calmed.

So quiet were the approaching Cheyenne and the troopers—who were downwind of the *tiospaye*—that the several dogs Fargo saw sprawled on the ground watching the women didn't so much as cock an ear or otherwise indicate they heard or smelled trouble brewing.

The warrior puckered and aimed his lips at the Cheyenne, then whispered, "War Chief Pony-Runs-Long."

Fargo's lake-blue eyes scanned the Cheyenne and stopped on the war bonnet that identified the man. A tall, powerfully built man, Pony-Runs-Long had a rawhide shield on his left forearm and a pogamoggan in his right hand. War paint covered his face as did all the other half-naked Cheyenne's. A warrior carrying a war staff adorned with many eagle feathers and scalps rode alongside the war chief. His free hand held both the hackamore reins and a carbine.

Fargo would have given anything to watch the two forces clash, if the Miniconju weren't caught in the middle. He pulled his Colt from its holster, checked to see that it was fully loaded, then did the same with his Sharps. He handed Crying Fox the Sharps and a palmful of cartridges and showed him how to eject spent shells and reload. Satisfied the warrior could operate the rifle, Fargo nodded, jammed his heels into the mighty stallion's flanks, and charged out of the tunnel. Crying Fox was right behind him. Fargo gave a loud war whoop as he burst from the canopy. Crying Fox did likewise, then added a warning, "*Hoka hey*! Cheyenne approach. *Hoka hey*, my brothers. Bluecoats approach."

The women froze in their tracks, took one fast look at the black-and-white horse and the big *wasicun* astride him, then grabbed up their babies and fled inside their tepees. The dogs ran barking and growling toward Fargo and Crying Fox. Warriors armed with bows and arrows spilled out the tepees and ran toward the corral.

As Fargo reined the Ovaro to a skidding halt on

the east bank of the pool and slipped from the saddle, the war chief broke out of the ground cover and led his screaming warriors into battle.

Simultaneously, the cannon roared. The cannonball hit in the center of the pool.

Fargo was drenched by the geyser it created. He wiped his eyes and saw the troopers riding low over their horses' necks, thundering in. He quickly gauged the distance separating the encampment from the two assaults and concluded the Cheyenne were closer, hence, the more immediate threat.

Crying Fox saw it, too. He flattened his belly on the ground and began firing at Cheyenne.

The cannon roared again. The gunnery officer had apparently adjusted its aim. The cannonball penetrated the thin covering on a tepee and exploded inside it. Two bodies were among the debris hurled high in the morning air. The tepee simply disintegrated; not a single pole remained standing.

Fargo stood and took aim on a Cheyenne warrior's chest. Moving from left to right, he shot six screaming warriors in the chest, reloaded, then shot two more before they scattered and the troopers arrived. By that time the Miniconju had made it to their ponies and joined the melee. The Cheyenne and Miniconju knew their differences, of course, and the one concentrated on the other. The troopers killed anyone not wearing a uniform. With the Cheyenne and Miniconju going for one another's throats, they made it easier for the troopers to torch the tepees. Fargo and Crying Fox continued shooting at war-painted faces.

An old woman staggered from a burning tepee near the east side of the pool. Fanning smoke off her face, she leaned on the tepee and hollered, "Where are you, white woman? Help me!"

Fargo was already sprinting to the old woman as he saw a head of blond hair poke out the tepee door flap, then the white woman crawl out.

"Help me, girl," the old woman continued to scream. "We must run and hide."

Pony-Runs-Long rode around the tepee and halted at the same time as Fargo got to the two females. The war chief swung his pogamoggan and bashed it into the old woman's head, killing her instantly.

Fargo aimed his Colt at the man's heart and squeezed the trigger, not once but twice, and the hammer fell on spent cartridges both times.

The war chief swung the pogamoggan against Fargo's gun hand. The Colt flew to the ground.

Fargo drew his Arkansas toothpick. Shifting into a crouch, he began dodging the fast-moving pogamoggan while trying to find an opening that would let him stab the pony-mounted man. He watched the big, round rock hanging at the bottom of rawhide thongs.

Pony-Runs-Long favored a backhand swing, Fargo noticed. After a backhand swing, the war chief would twist his wrist and for an instant the weight of the deadly rock would cause it to become immobile. Fargo waited for a backhand and twist, then shot his free hand out, grabbed the thongs, and yanked the pogamoggan out of Pony-Runs-Long's grip. He flung the mace into the dirt and stabbed for the Indian's gut.

The war chief blocked the thrust with his shield, sliding off his pony at the same time.

The white woman shrieked and pointed behind Fargo.

He glimpsed a war-painted face and an onrushing tomahawk in the nick of time to fall to his left. The sharp blade of the tomahawk missed his head by an inch. The warrior wasn't so lucky. Fargo's stiletto rammed into the warrior's belly and sliced it wide open. The stunned warrior sank to his knees.

Fargo turned to take on Pony-Runs-Long, but the war chief had mounted up and ridden away. Fargo was too much for him. The Miniconju were easier adversaries, much easier.

Fargo retrieved his empty Colt, then grabbed the blonde by a wrist and pulled her to her feet. "Come on," he bellowed over the gunfire. He dragged her stumbling toward the pool. On the way he saw Crying

Fox swinging the Sharps by its barrel at two pony-mounted Cheyenne warriors who were crowding him into a burning tepee. He told the blonde, "Run and jump into the pool."

The frantic woman did as he said.

Fargo ran to help his friend. He didn't bother loading the Colt. "Cold steel is what they deserve," he muttered, and pulled one of the warriors off his pony. Fargo stabbed him in the heart. Crying Fox slammed the stock of the Sharps a bone-crushing blow to the other warrior's head. Blood gushed from the new part in the warrior's braided hair. The victim fell to the ground and lay there groaning lowly. Fargo handed the stiletto to Crying Fox, who put the wounded warrior out of his misery.

"Follow me into the pool," Fargo yelled. "There's nothing we can do to help."

Crying Fox reluctantly did as Fargo suggested.

The three of them kept their eyes above the surface and watched the fracas. Sabers flashed, pistols and carbines barked, bowstrings twanged, and arrows flew continuously. It was fighting from close quarters, extremely close. The troopers were having a field day with so many red targets. All the tepees were blazing now. The confused dogs no longer recognized friend from foe. They snapped and bit indiscriminately.

A lieutenant spotted the three heads in the pool. With saber in hand, he charged to lop them off. As he came closer, Fargo rose from the water and pointed the now-loaded Colt at him. The officer tried halting the bay mare he rode, but couldn't stop her short of the pool. The mare plunged into the water alongside Fargo. Fargo grabbed the lieutenant's saber arm and pulled him off his saddle.

The lieutenant thrashed about in the water, trying to get his footing and cussing, "Goddamned mare! She won't whoa when I order. I'll have to shoot her yet."

"Name's Skye Fargo," the big man holding him up said.

"Were you going to shoot me?" the officer asked, a hint of disbelief in his voice.

"I would have if you hadn't halted," Fargo replied wryly.

The officer regained his footing on the sandy bottom and started to get back on the bay. When Fargo pulled him away, he spun around and yelled, "Unhand me, man! I have my orders, and I intend to carry them out."

"Oh? And what might those orders be?" Fargo asked quite calmly.

"Punish the Sioux savages," the lieutenant snarled.

Fargo grabbed the front of the man's tunic, pulled his face close to his, and growled, "Does punishment include murder?"

Struggling to wrench free, the lieutenant quipped halfheartedly, "Mister, they're nothing but ignorant savages."

Fargo raised him out of the water and threw a hard fist against the misguided, misinformed officer's jaw, and discovered it was made of glass. The one blow knocked out the lieutenant. Fargo pulled the unconscious body to where the pool shallowed and left him faceup there.

He removed cartridges for the Sharps from his gun belt and gave them to Crying Fox. "Load and fire at war-painted faces and any bluecoats you see threatening Miniconju, especially women and children."

Crying Fox left the pool to kneel on its bank and fire. Fargo stood in waist-deep water to do the same. In short order they downed seven men with long shots. Fargo shot three Cheyenne warriors, Crying Fox two others and two troopers chasing down women.

A bugle sounded, calling for the troopers to break off their attack and return to the depression. They reluctantly obeyed the bugler. As they broke and rode away, Fargo saw the Cheyenne were now outnumbered by Miniconju warriors. Pony-Runs-Long realized it, too. He gave the Cheyenne warriors the

24

command to disengage and fall back. Miniconju arrows ensured their retreat.

Fargo turned to the blonde and asked, "You are Elvira Blassingame, the preacher's daughter, aren't you?"

"Why, yes, I am," she drawled in a thick southern accent. "And how might you know my name and that I am a preacher's daughter?"

"Brother Blassingame himself told me. We can get out of the water now. It's safe. My friend Crying Fox will tell his Miniconju brothers not to shoot us." Fargo gestured for Crying Fox to clear the way for them, then pulled the officer ashore.

Elvira stood and walked ashore. Her dripping-wet buckskin dress clung to her shapely body like a fresh coat of tan paint. It was as though she stood naked before Fargo. The bodice of the dress formed around and accentuated her full breasts before plunging over her flat abdomen. Even the indented belly button showed. When she turned to face a burning tepee, Fargo clearly saw the nice shape of her ass. The tightly clinging dress dipped into the crack between her buttock cheeks and left little for Fargo to imagine.

Elvira stood about five-foot-six. Fargo reckoned she weighed no more than 120 pounds. But it was her face that captivated him. He preferred women having a square jawline, especially when they had full, wide lips like Elvira's. She also had warm clear brown eyes, not that he overlooked her pert, upturned nose. He wondered if she would prove to be the haughty, untouchable type, or if a hellcat simmered just beneath all the clear, unblemished skin.

The officer stirred and broke Fargo's fixation on the blonde. Fargo slapped him into full consciousness.

Checking his hurt jaw, the lieutenant mumbled, "What happened? Is the fight still going on?"

"No," Fargo muttered. "It's over and everyone went home."

The lieutenant rolled over and propped up on one elbow to view the dead and destruction. Then he

25

noticed Elvira and asked, "A white woman dressed like an Indian? Where did you come from, ma'am?"

She glanced at him, smiled as she offered, "Around."

Fargo explained, "Her name is Elvira Blassingame. She was taken from a wagon train three months ago by War Chief Pony-Runs-Long, the same man who carried out the massacre of settlers on the wagon train that prompted McRae to issue your orders."

"General McRae," the lieutenant corrected as he stood on wobbly legs.

"Whatever," Fargo replied sardonically. "Idiocy knows no rank. Even generals are sometimes affected with it." He added with a touch of sarcasm, "You prove that."

The lieutenant balled his fists and snapped rather curtly, as though dressing down a dumb country-boy private in his cups, "Listen here, mister, you'd be wise to—"

Elvira interrupted him, blurting, "See here, Lieutenant. Don't you go censuring the man who saved my life and probably a dozen others, including yours. My word, is fighting and killing all you think about?"

The officer ignored her. Looking about, he asked, "Where is the detachment? I must get back to it. Where's my horse?"

The mare had left the pool. She now grazed left of the corral, swishing flies off her rump and hind legs with her tail.

Fargo pointed to her and said, "Your detachment, what was left of it, headed north."

"I must get to them," the lieutenant repeated.

Fargo chuckled, then spoke evenly. "No, Lieutenant, you're going to Fort Laramie with Elvira and me. If necessary, I'll force you to go at gunpoint. Hand me your revolver."

"Aw, shit," the young lieutenant lamented as he handed Fargo the gun. "I feel naked without my saber. Where is it? Anybody seen it?"

Elvira shook her head.

Fargo answered, "It's on the bottom in the deepest part of the pool. You won't be needing it, though. I'll tell the general where he can find it. Come on. I see Crying Fox trying to catch my attention."

They followed him to Crying Fox, who stood conversing with three warriors.

Fargo asked, "What is it, Crying Fox?"

The warriors looked at the lieutenant.

Crying Fox told him, "Bluecoat, you caused great trouble this morning. Don't you know right from wrong? The headman lies dead, blown to pieces by the iron giant on wheels. So does the medicine man, Sleeping Bull Buffalo. So do sixteen other of my brothers and sisters and little ones. Look around you, Bluecoat, and tell us what you see."

The officer refused to look at the many bodies on the ground or the complete destruction of the *tiospaye*. Instead, he said, "I had my orders."

Fargo interpreted. The warriors became restless and angry. It showed in their widened eyes and on their faces. Fargo suggested, "We better leave before they scalp all three of us." Then to the warriors he said, "We go now. I will tell General McRae at Fort Laramie to stop the killing. I need this officer and white woman to support me; otherwise the general won't believe my word. He will keep on killing your people with the iron giant. I will need to borrow a pony for the woman to ride."

Crying Fox saw the wisdom of letting them go. He told his companions, "The big *wasicun* can be trusted to say to this general what he has told us. I say let them go. Do you agree?"

One by one Fargo watched the warriors nod. "Ride fast, *mi kola*," Crying Fox suggested to Fargo. "Tell this general at Fort Laramie the Sioux are not his enemy. The Cheyenne are. Tell him there will be no peace until Pony-Runs-Long is dead. Tell him that, my friend. Now you go." He handed Elvira the reins to a pony.

The lieutenant hurried to his horse.

Fargo whistled for the Ovaro. He trotted to him with ears perked. Elvira hiked the hem of her dress, leapt onto the pony's bare back, then nodded she was ready to ride. Fargo eased up into his saddle and gestured to the lieutenant for him to meet them at the opening of the downstream canopy. Then he nudged the stallion into a walk and went there.

On the way Elvira looked over her shoulder and commented, "I'll miss that old, wrinkle-faced woman. She was good to me. So gentle and kind."

Fargo said, "I know. Most of them are. How did the Cheyenne treat you?"

Elvira muttered, "You wouldn't want to know," and said no more.

The lieutenant caught up to them in the tunnel. He was still concerned about his detachment. "Sure as hell they're going to get lost without me. Lieutenant Ross doesn't know c'mere from sicc'um about navigating out in the wide open spaces. He's new to the plains. Ross gets lost anytime he can't see the fort. I don't know why McRae assigned him to me."

Too late the lieutenant realized he'd made a faux pas.

Fargo chuckled first, then said most wryly, "It's *General* McRae. And you just called him an idiot. By the way, Lieutenant, what is your name?"

"Hollowell, sir. Max Hollowell. Lieutenant Maxwell Hollowell."

Fargo said, "Not to worry, Hollowell. Your detachment will wander a day or two, then a sergeant will find a way to aim Lieutenant Ross in the direction of Fort Laramie. They'll ride into the fort all haggard and worn out. That same night they will lie on their cots and tell their buddies they left behind all about war, how fierce Sioux women and children fought them, and how they were forced to kill them. Lieutenant Ross will brag also, only he will be sitting at the officer's mess table when he does. He'll give all the junior officers the benefit of his experience in the art

28

of bombarding tepees. You do have junior officers, don't you, Hollowell?"

Max didn't answer.

At high noon eleven days later they rode through the gates of Fort Laramie. A raging summer rainstorm had been with them since before daybreak. They were tired, hungry, and sleepy.

"Where is the general's office?" Fargo asked the lieutenant in a testy tone of voice. Max hadn't spoken in the last two days, and he was wearing thin on Fargo's patience.

Now he did. Pointing through the downpour, he shouted over a loud clap of thunder, "Over there . . . I think."

They crossed the muddy parade grounds and reined to a halt in front of a two-story, stone-and-mortar building. Lamplight spilled through the open doorway and windows on the ground floor.

Fargo dismounted and lifted Elvira off her Indian pony.

Hollowell dismounted quickly and strode through the doorway in advance of Fargo and Elvira, who sauntered inside the general's office in time to see Max salute smartly and hear him say, "Sir, Lieutenant Hollowell reporting, sir."

McRae, a bull of a man, in his fifties, leaned to one end of his desk and looked around Max, who stood ramrod-straight and maintained his salute, to see who followed the lieutenant inside. The cigar jutting from one corner of his mouth nearly fell out when he saw Elvira. In a mellow baritone voice that would charm most folks, he asked, "What are you doing here, young lady?"

Fargo watched McRae's gaze move down and back up Elvira's shapeliness, made even more provocative by the wet, clinging dress and the way she stood, weight on her left foot, hand on her right hip; McRae saw what Fargo saw, the nice contours of the woman's body.

Fargo answered, "She's with me, General."

McRae's gaze shifted to Fargo. "And who are you?"

"Skye Fargo. Some call me the Trailsman."

The general leaned back in his chair. Fargo thought he gave a half-assed salute—it was nothing to compare with the lieutenant's crisply executed one—to Max Hollowell, saying at the same time, "Stand at ease, Lieutenant. Now you can report."

Max held his salute.

Taking a step closer to the desk, Fargo broke in before Hollowell could answer. "General, can the report wait until after the young lady's needs are taken care of?"

McRae snorted, "Harumph! Yes, certainly." He became restless, shifted in his chair twice, toyed absent-mindedly with items on the desk.

Fargo realized he had embarrassed the man. McRae wasn't accustomed to having females around, especially in his office. The general probably did not know anything about a woman's needs. Fargo pointed out a few. "She's tired, General. Exhausted, in fact. She needs a hot bath followed by a hot meal, then sleep. When she awakens, Elvira will need clean, dry clothing."

McRae didn't reply right off because he was staring, frowning at Max Hollowell. Max had a pained expression on his face and was still rigid as a statue, holding the salute. McRae said, "Are you blind, Lieutenant? Didn't you see me return your salute and hear me tell you to stand easy?"

"Yes, sir."

"Then what's your problem?"

"Sir, all the blood has drained out of my right arm. I can't move it, sir. It's locked in place."

Fargo stepped to him and bent Max's right arm straight out, then shoved it down to the man's side. Hollowell groaned his relief. He wiggled his hand and fingers to start the blood flowing again.

The general shouted, "Brice! Brice, get in here."

A side door swung open. A tall, lanky sergeant with close-cropped red hair and a mustache so long it curved to his chin stepped into the room. "You hollered for me, General?" Brice tensed when he saw Elvira. She flashed him a winsome smile.

"Quit ogling, Sergeant," McRae ordered. "The young lady needs a hot bath, followed by a hot meal, then sleep. When she awakens, she will need clean clothing. Tend to her needs, Sergeant."

Fargo pursed his lips and raised his eyebrows. The general had repeated him almost verbatim.

Brice's body language revealed his discomfort with McRae's order. The sergeant looked alternately from Elvira to the general as he stammered, "Er, ah, sir, how, sir? Where?"

"Improvise, Sergeant. Improvise. A seasoned soldier such as yourself should know how to cope with the unexpected. Stay fluid, Sergeant. You'll figure it out."

Brice's shoulders sagged. He headed for the front door, saying, "Follow me, ma'am." Then he muttered loud enough for Fargo to hear, "The boys in A Barracks are going to get the surprise of their life."

Elvira followed him through the doorway.

McRae gestured for Fargo to sit. He slouched in the only other chair in the room, a straight-back. Steepling his fingers, McRae looked at Hollowell. "You were about to say?"

With his hands clasped firmly at the small of his back, Max parted his feet a tad and launched into his report. "The detachment punished the Sioux, sir, starting one day's ride north of the fort, then continuing north into the Montana Territory. Six encampments in all were destroyed, sir."

"How many men did you lose?" McRae cut in to ask.

Hollowell gulped. In a pained voice he admitted, "I don't know, sir."

The only sound interrupting the otherwise heavy silence in the room was made by a big horsefly buzzing to land on one corner of the desk. Finally, McRae asked in a tone laced with controlled disbelief, "You don't know? You do know how many rode through the front gate when you left?"

"Oh, yes, sir. Thirty-two, sir . . . and one cannon."

"Then I suggest you step outside and count how many came back. Simple subtraction will tell you how many men you lost in battle."

Fargo broke his silence by chuckling. "The lieutenant can't do that, General. Because there are no troopers or cannon outside." When McRae furrowed his brow and looked questioningly at both of them, the Trailsman moved to stand beside Max. Fargo explained, "I knocked out the lieutenant during a combined Cheyenne and army attack on a Miniconju *tiospaye* just inside Montana Territory. The attack was over and everyone had left before Hollowell regained consciousness." He paused intentionally to give General McRae time to wrestle with and sort out the problem. Fargo suspected McRae, like the lieutenant, was new to the frontier.

McRae stood. His face was beet-red as he bit into the cigar. He started pacing, first moving to the front door, then behind Hollowell and back to the doorway again, where he stood looking out at the downpour. He slapped a balled fist several times into his open palm at the small of his back. Without turning he said, "Lieutenant, you're dismissed."

Max glanced over his shoulder at him. "Sir, I, I, uh—"

"Goddammit, Lieutenant, are you deaf, too?" McRae interrupted. And Fargo detected murder in his tone. "I'll take care of you later. Right now I want to speak privately with this man."

Max snapped to attention, saluted, did an about-face, then fled around the general and out into the rain. Fargo and McRae watched him march across the muddy parade ground until swallowed in the torrential downpour. Fargo heard the general sigh heavily, saw his broad shoulders sag slightly. McRae shook his head. Turning, he said, "This is my first assignment outside of Washington." He walked behind his desk and sat before continuing. "I don't belong here. Did I hear correct? You did say a combined Cheyenne and army attack?"

Fargo pulled the straight-back close to the desk. He answered as he sat. "You heard correct. Let me explain why I was there. Six weeks ago I was leaving Portland, Oregon, when I met a wagon train heading toward that city. I learned from the wagon master that a young woman—the one you have Sergeant Brice looking after—had been captured by Indians north of your fort."

"I didn't know," McRae interjected. "I assumed command on the Fourth of July. Go on."

"It happened two weeks prior to that time. Anyhow, the incident wasn't reported. The wagon train continued to Oregon. The wagon master took me to the couple whose daughter had been taken, a Baptist preacher and his wife from Atlanta, Georgia. I told Obidiah and Catherine—"

"Catherine was my wife's name," McRae interrupted. "She was from New Orleans. Lovely woman."

Fargo noted the past tense. From the wistful look in the officer's dark eyes, he presumed Catherine McRae was deceased. Fargo continued, "Anyhow I told them that inasmuch as I was going that way, I'd search for their daughter. Obidiah said they were settling in Seattle and he gave me the address of the church."

Again McRae broke into Fargo's story, this time to ask, "You would do that for complete strangers? Why, Mr. Fargo? Why would you place your life in jeopardy, ride straight into hostile territory?"

Fargo chuckled. "I know most of the Indians living between the Mississippi and the Pacific, and from Mexico to Canada. The bad and the good. I speak enough of their language to get by. Especially the three Sioux dialects."

"What do you do, exactly, Mr. Fargo? By that I

mean your line of work? Fur-trader? Prospector? You appear to be neither."

Fargo shook his head. "I don't have a line of work, General. Neither do I have a home—at least not a regular home. The wilderness is my home. From time to time I accept commissions to perform specific tasks, such as searching for someone. The preacher paid me two hundred dollars to find Elvira."

"That's interesting," McRae mused. "Back to your story."

"While searching for Elvira, I came across Lakota encampments destroyed by Lieutenant Hollowell's men and the iron giant on wheels."

"Iron giant on wheels?" McRae asked. He frowned.

"That's what the Indians call the cannon. Friendly Lakota, people whose word I could trust to be accurate, told me you were punishing them wrongfully."

"Oh? Those redskins lied, Mr. Fargo. They were interrupting commerce, killing whites, stealing, and so on. I had no choice."

"No, General, you did have a choice. For inst—"

"They were hostile savages, Mr. Fargo," McRae thundered.

The man's attitude, his constant interruptions, and his total lack of knowledge of the Indians, especially the Lakota, were wearing Fargo's patience mighty thin. Somebody had obviously passed command to the general without adequately preparing him. Fargo leaned on the desk and growled, "Shut up, General, and listen. The Indians were here first. You and I are the interlopers."

McRae winced. He muttered defensively, "Yes, but, but—"

"No buts about it," Fargo began in a calmer tone. "The Lakota didn't disrupt any commerce. The Cheyenne did. Specifically, War Chief Pony-Runs-Long. Most Cheyenne are peaceable. Pony-Runs-Long is a renegade. The Lakota paid dearly for what Pony-Runs-Long did. He took Elvira from the wagon train. During a night raid to steal Cheyenne women, Miniconju warriors stole her by mistake. Crying Fox, a Sans Arc warrior, had heard that a white woman who fit Elvira's description was in a Miniconju *tiospaye*." When McRae's brow furrowed, Fargo explained, "A *tiospaye* is an encampment of close relatives—a clan, if you will. They vary in size, ranging from a few tepees upward to many, depending solely on the hunting territory decided on for each at the annual Council of the Seven Fires."

"You know a lot, Mr. Fargo. Please continue." McRae seemed genuinely interested.

Fargo relaxed, leaned back in his chair, and went on. "When Crying Fox and I arrived at the Miniconju encampment, we saw Pony-Runs-Long's warriors moving into position to attack from one side, and Lieutenant Hollowell's troopers from the other. Neither group was aware of the other. Then all hell broke loose. Even the dogs were taken by surprise."

Fargo went on to recount the fight and the confusion created. "The last I saw of the detachment it was hightailing it to the north. Some of the troopers got killed. I shot several myself. They were murdering indiscriminately. I shot only those who directly threatened Miniconju.

"After it was over, I threatened to bring back Lieutenant Hollowell at gunpoint, if necessary. The three of us got the hell out of there before the Miniconju survivors could collect their wits. Elvira will confirm Pony-Runs-Long is responsible for terrorizing the commerce of which you speak."

"Where is the detachment?" McRae wondered aloud. "Washington will have my ass when it learns of this." Glancing up from his fingers drumming on the top of the desk, he changed the subject abruptly. "Mr. Fargo, I have a daughter about the same age as Miss Blassingame."

Fargo waited.

"She, too, is a lovely young woman. I am a widower, Mr. Fargo. Catherine, God rest her soul, died from consumption only this past April, when the cherry trees at the nation's capital were in full bloom. We buried her in a cemetery where cherry trees grow. Catherine adored the blossoms."

Sergeant Brice strode into the office and broke the general's train of thought. To Fargo, Brice resembled a drowning rat with a half-assed smile on its face. Brice explained, "General, your orders have been carried out. If you will dismiss me, sir, I will step into the other room and change clothes."

McRae flicked a hand to dismiss him. When the door closed behind Brice, the general picked back up where he had left off before the interruption. "Regina is my daughter's name. After Catherine passed away, I suppose General Tate at the War Department decided I could use a different duty assignment. Tate's and my family were very close, Mr. Fargo. I know his intentions were honorable when he gave me the command at Fort Laramie. In truth, I needed to get away from Washington. I visited Catherine's grave every day. Tate knew I was grieving over losing her. So when Colonel Brandenberg made brigadier, Tate assigned him to become his aide and sent me to Fort Laramie. Tate said it would be for a year only."

When he paused and a faraway look showed in his eyes, Fargo coughed discreetly.

It was sufficient to jerk the general back into the present. McRae said, "Where was I?"

"You were saying the assignment would be for a year."

"Yes," McRae intoned in a stronger voice. "For a year. Regina accompanied me. I didn't know what I was getting her into. Hell, I didn't know what I was getting myself into. Tate claimed the assignment would be routine stuff, meaning shuffling paperwork, holding dress parades, and the like. The closer Regina and I got to Fort Laramie, the more I realized that Tate was wrong. Tate's never been west of the Mississippi River. So he really didn't know what it would be like for my Regina out here on the edge of civilization. En route we passed half-naked savages with feathers in their hair and holding tomahawks or clubs. It wasn't anything like Tate had said."

"You received a good dose of culture shock," Fargo said.

"Yes, well, when we arrived here, I knew at once this was no place for Regina. She was reared in Washington society. Hunh, society doesn't exist out here. We talked about her returning to Washington. I would join her after my tour is complete. Regina told me she didn't want to go back to Washington. We talked about that. One thing led to another. We weren't getting anywhere on the matter."

Fargo wished he'd hurry up and make his point. He encouraged the general by inquiring, "Where is your daughter now?"

"I'm getting to that. Regina said she would like to spend the year visiting her Aunt Fontaine in New Orleans. I agreed. Sarah Fontaine and her husband, Jules, own a shipping business. Exports and imports. They could introduce Regina to New Orleans society. It was decided Regina would visit with the Fontaines. She left with a patrol I assigned to guard her the next day, July eighth. The patrol escorted her to St. Louis and saw to it that she secured passage on a steamboat. Regina never made it to New Orleans."

"Oh? Why? Don't tell me the boat sank."

"No, Mr. Fargo, the *Gypsy Queen* didn't run aground, blow up, or sink. The last anyone saw of Regina was the night before the vessel docked at Memphis. Regina simply disappeared."

"Did the authorities look for her? Maybe she got off the boat without anyone noticing, went into town, and—"

"No, Mr. Fargo," McRae hastened to cut in, "Regina didn't leave the *Gypsy Queen*. The captain, a Mr. Fogg, told the authorities he watched those who did leave and Regina wasn't among them. Neither did she have breakfast either in her stateroom or in the dining salon. Fogg thought it odd, seeing how she'd never missed attending breakfast. Fogg went to her stateroom. He found the door ajar and promptly investigated. While Regina's bed had been slept in, she was missing. Fogg reports the dress she wore at dinner was draped over the back of a chair. A search was made of her wardrobe. Nothing appeared missing."

"Maybe she fell overboard."

"That's not within the realm of possibility, Mr. Fargo."

"Why so?"

"Because, Mr. Fargo, Regina sleeps nude. Catherine detested the habit. She often warned Regina it would one day invite trouble. Regina would never appear on deck stark-naked. Her petticoat and pantaloons were also on the chair."

Fargo silently disagreed with McRae. Why wouldn't the young woman take a nocturnal stroll on deck? Made good sense to Skye Fargo. He said, "Perhaps somebody threw her overboard."

"I think not, Mr. Fargo. Will you accept a commission to find Regina?"

obord. He.to.its the door.tus. and promptly loves.
ped. When Fargo a bed had been slept in, she was
attached out into r blue dress, cut, was as fingers r.s
draped over the-but of a chair A which was the
edher-tenable-no-thing-memed r-this-she aw.

3

The pleading in the general's eyes conveyed to Fargo the man's feeling of helplessness in this situation. McRae was trapped, more or less confined to the fort. His only child was missing, and he could do absolutely nothing but wonder about her fate. Fargo imagined him lying awake at night, trying to understand her disappearance. No wonder, Fargo thought, the man commits errors in judgment. It preys on his mind constantly.

Fargo said, "I'll have to talk with Elvira first. I told the Blassingames that when I found her, I'd personally escort their daughter to Seattle."

McRae nodded solemnly.

They sat awhile longer, saying nothing. Fargo listened to the rain tattooing on the roof. He suspected the general didn't hear it or anything else. McRae's mind was in a different place, either at the grave or on board the *Gypsy Queen*, probably bouncing between the two.

Finally Fargo spoke. "Well, General, I have to look after my horse."

The comment jerked McRae out of his reverie. He blinked and said, "Use the fort's stable, Mr. Fargo. Sergeant Brice will take you to it, then fix you up with a place to sleep. Please join me and my officers for dinner." He turned to holler for Brice.

Fargo stopped the order in time. "No need for the sergeant to get wet a second time. I know my way around the fort. And I accept your invitation to dine with you. Besides, your officers have a better brand of bourbon." He shot McRae a wink, pushed away from the desk, and sauntered outside.

McRae followed him as far as the doorway. As Fargo mounted up, the general lamented, "If it isn't raining, it's baking hot. Dinner is at five o'clock."

Fargo nodded, then wheeled the Ovaro and rode to the stable. A corporal met him at the entrance. Looking at the rain clouds, he spat a stream of tobacco juice, then drawled, "Regular frog-strangler where I come from. Come on in, mister. Nice-looking animal you have there. Them jet-black fore- and hind-quarters and white midsection sure do gleam. Wouldn't want to part with him, I suppose?"

Fargo dismounted. "Not for sale or trade, Corporal."

"Just my luck. Follow me and I'll show you the stall."

They chatted while going to the stall at the rear of the barn. Fargo remarked, "What's a southern gent doing way out here?"

The corporal chuckled. "Beats hell out of me. It's a far piece from Kentucky, though. I miss the flat kind of water, not the falling-down kind, like what's coming down outside. Name's Peters. Orly Peters. Most call me Pete. Yours?"

"Skye Fargo."

"Ain't you the one who brought Lieutenant Hollowell back?"

Fargo nodded.

"When he brought his mare to me, he said you were with the general. Hollowell—er, Lieutenant Hollowell, that is, said you took him away from his detachment and left Lieutenant Ross in charge. That true?"

"I did. What else did he volunteer?"

"Said you brought a pretty woman, too."

"That's so. Where is she?"

"I dunno. Brice took her somewhere. The lieutenant didn't say."

Fargo changed the subject. "Flat kind of water? I take it you mean a river."

"That's right. The Ohio. I was born on the Kentucky side. Don't suppose you ever heard of Cave-in Rock?"

Fargo shook his head.

"This is the stall. Get him in. I'll go get some army oats."

Fargo removed his bedroll and saddlebags and draped them over the gate. The corporal returned with a bucketful of oats while Fargo was removing the saddle. Orly picked up on his earlier reference to Cave-in Rock. "Bad place that Cave-in Rock. I could see it from our farm on the bank of the Ohio. Pirates used it as their hideout a long time ago. Pa told me that. Nice-looking Sharps you got there. Wouldn't want—"

"Not for sale or trade," Fargo interrupted. He removed the bridle and reins. The Ovaro didn't need encouragement to partake of the army's oats. Fargo closed the stall gate and reached for the gear on top of it.

"Here, lemme carry that bedding for you," Orly offered.

Handing it to him, Fargo asked, "Ever see the steamboat *Gypsy Queen* on the Ohio?"

"Once, when I was a kid. I think she runs 'tween St. Louie and New Orleans now."

They walked back to the entrance. Looking out, Fargo inquired, "Pete, are any of the pirates still around?"

"If you mean at Cave-in Rock, no. But they're still around. On the Mississip', I hear tell. Pa told me that, too. Pa said Little Harpe cut off Captain Samuel Mason's head for a nine-hundred-dollar reward. Mason was the ringleader of the pirates. Pa said after Mason lost his head, the pirates broke up. But some of them are still around. Pickpockets, card-cheating gamblers, thieves, and the like. They'll do anything for a dollar."

"Steal people?"

"That, too. Well, bless my soul, it's fixing to stop raining. Where are you bunking down tonight?"

41

"Do you have any place particular in mind? I'm not choosy."

"B Barracks. That's where I live." He pointed at the barracks.

Fargo nodded and headed that way. Inside the barracks he put his stuff on a barren bed. Four soldiers stripped to the waist played cards at a table. Two others propped up in their beds wrote letters. Fargo stepped to the table and asked one of the men where he could find an army towel and washrag. Without glancing up from his poker hand, the fellow pointed to a stack of folded towels on a chest. Fargo found the washrags next to the stack. He took one of each to the barracks washroom. He stripped and began bathing the stink off his muscular body. A few minutes later one of the letter-writers came in and used the porcelain washbowl two stations down from him. Fargo asked, "Where is everyone? This place looks like a ghost town."

The man answered dryly, "Chasing hostiles. If Gump and me weren't running fevers at the time they left, we'd be with them. Lucky us."

"Lieutenant Hollowell's detachment?"

"Yeah. Know him?"

"We've met. What does the barracks think about him?" Fargo asked, because he knew the troopers had long since figured out Hollowell's level of expertise. What the barracks thought of the man was probably a true assessment.

The trooper summed it up with one word: "Reckless."

"Lieutenant Ross?"

"Greenhorn."

The fellow was good at summation. He was also accurate. "And the general?"

"We haven't figured McRae out yet. One day he's all spit and polish, goes by the book, and the next he acts as though he simply doesn't give a shit. What're you doing here?"

"I escorted the lieutenant back to the fort."

The soldier stopped washing his face. He looked at the big man with keen interest as he said, "So you're the one. Brice told us you and Hollowell and a good-looking woman dressed in buckskin were in with the general. Brice also said the detachment wasn't back yet."

Fargo knew the troopers burned with curiosity to learn what really happened. He threw the man a bone. "Hollowell lost his sword during an attack on a Miniconju encampment." Out the corner of his eye Fargo saw the soldier blink.

Nothing more was said. The trooper dried his face, then hurried out of the washroom. Fargo knew his last statement would spread like wildfire from barracks to barracks. He finished bathing, toweled dry, picked up his wet clothes, and went back into the barracks.

The card game had ended. One of the players was missing. Probably spreading the word, Fargo mused to himself. He laid out his clothing to dry on the slats of the bed next to his, opened his bedroll, and reclined on it. He fell asleep quickly.

A bugle call awakened him. He found the barracks deserted. Reaching for his underwear, he found they had dried. The shirt and Levi's were still damp, but acceptable. He dressed and stepped into the doorway. The troopers and their officers stood at attention on the parade grounds. All faced the American flag, which was being lowered. Fargo waited until the flag had been folded and the men dismissed before he ambled toward the officer's mess hall across the parade grounds.

Stepping inside the room, he saw McRae and two other officers already seated at a dining table. As he crossed to the general's table, all talk ceased and the officers seated around the other tables looked at the big man. Fargo sat in the vacant chair between McRae and a colonel.

McRae made the introductions. Glancing to the colonel, he said, "Mr. Fargo, my aide, Lieutenant Colonel Seymore." Seymore nodded. McRae looked at the other officer. "Major Gatewood." Gatewood nodded.

Fargo didn't see Lieutenant Hollowell. He presumed the man had been confined to quarters.

McRae explained he had brought Seymore with him from Washington. Major Gatewood followed two weeks later from Fort Apache, where he had served as second-in-command for two years. Fargo instantly realized Gatewood alone represented all of the strength at this table. Why, then, he wondered, did McRae assign Lieutenant Hollowell to lead the detachment and not Gatewood? The army moves in mysterious ways, he decided.

Spic-and-span orderlies served the meal—roast beef and trimmings—then departed to stand nearby and wait until time to clear the tables. Little conversation transpired at Fargo's table while they ate, and then only between him and the major.

Gatewood, obviously interested, asked, "General McRae tells me you know the Sioux."

"Yes. I am a blood brother."

"He also tells me you contend Cheyenne were responsible for the attacks on wagon trains, not the Sioux."

"That's correct. Specifically, War Chief Pony-Runs-Long. The man is a renegade. Not all Cheyenne agree with his vow to kill as many whites as he can."

"I see," said Gatewood, and said no more until the orderlies had cleared the table and served drinks.

McRae lit a fresh cigar and got comfortable. Sipping from a glass of whiskey, he looked at Gatewood, who asked Fargo, "Where, exactly, do you suggest I find Pony-Runs-Long?"

The major's tone made it clear McRae had decided to not only trust Fargo's word but also send his most-seasoned officer to stop the Cheyenne war chief. Smart move, Fargo thought, but said, "Pony-Runs-Long ranges all along the edge of Sioux territory from upper Wyoming deep into Montana Territory. Unfortunately he has no fixed position. The Lakota want him as badly as you do. I suggest you make friends with the Lakota. I can promise they will ride with you once they know you come in peace and intend to put an end to the man."

"They would do that? Ride with me?"

"Certainly." Fargo glanced at McRae and added, "But only after you smoke their pipes in peace with them. Heaven help you if you break your word. The Sioux have long memories." He took a sip of bourbon.

"About how many warriors ride with Pony-Runs-Long?" Gatewood asked.

"Right now less than the thirty I saw at the Miniconju *tiospaye*. Between your people, the Miniconju, and myself we thinned the war chief's numbers. But you can rest assured he will muster other Cheyenne to make up the losses. He's probably already done it."

McRae changed the subject. "Have you talked with Miss Blassingame?"

"No," Fargo answered. "I haven't seen her since she left your office."

McRae nodded. The conversation drifted to discussing Washington. Fargo found it boring. At the first opportunity he excused himself. Pushing back from the table, he said, "Gentlemen, I take my leave. My belly is full of roast beef—I thank you for a fine meal. The cooks are to be complimented."

McRae and the others started to rise. Fargo said, "Don't get up. Please continue your conversation." He knew the officers treasured this time of the day and wanted to chat over drinks. McRae and the colonel would reminisce about the social life in Washington for hours. Fargo didn't want to hear it. He left.

Few troopers were in B Barracks. The letter-writer told Fargo most of the men were bellied up to the bar in Rockerby's Saloon in Laramie. Fargo undressed and snuggled inside his bedroll. He drifted into sleep wondering where Elvira slept and what had happened to Regina McRae.

He awakened in predawn, dressed, and went outside. Lamps burned in the soldier's mess hall. Like a moth, he was drawn to the lamplight spilling through the windows. Coming close to the building, he smelled the aroma of coffee. He went inside, helped himself to a cup of the brew, then sat at a long table to drink it while listening to the cooks chat among themselves.

He was working on his third cup of coffee when Elvira walked in grinning. Fargo laughed so hard that he sloshed coffee all over the tabletop. Elvira looked ridiculous dressed in baggy, oversized uniform trousers and shirt a big trooper had obviously furnished. The pant legs were rolled up at least four inches, the cuffs of the shirt hid her hands, and if it weren't for the army-issue suspenders, her pants would have fallen to the floor. On her head rested a bugler's hat cocked at an angle. A pair of much-used army boots completed her ensemble.

She sat beside him and drawled, "I had a helluva night."

Fargo burst out laughing again. "I bet you did. Want some coffee?"

"Need it desperately."

He got up, filled two cups, and handed her one. Sitting, he asked, "What happened? Where did you get that outfit?" He belly-laughed again.

Grinning, Elvira poked his upper left arm. "Don't make fun, Fargo. At least they are dry and clean. A bugler gave me the clothes. You don't want to know what happened."

That made twice Fargo had heard her use the phrase. It was obviously her way of saying she had gotten screwed. He didn't probe for additional information. Turning serious, he told her about Regina McRae's disappearance and the general's offer of a commission. Fargo concluded by saying, "I told him I would have to talk to you first. I don't know whether or not you will agree to the delay in my taking you to Seattle. You have first priority on my movements."

Elvira was already shaking her head before he finished the last part of the statement. "No, Fargo, I don't want to go to Seattle. For the life of me, I don't know why I let Daddy and Mama talk me into going with them in the first place. What happened on the way only proves I wasn't supposed to go. That old Miniconju woman told me that. She said the spirits were looking out for my best interests. An English-speaking warrior interpreted for her. He said I should listen to my heart."

"You're positive you don't want to go?"

"Positive."

"Then I will send a message by the next Pony Express rider headed for Sacramento for further relay to the church in Seattle. In your own words you can tell your parents your decision. Do you want to remain in Laramie?"

"No. I'm not cut out for life on the frontier. I don't know where I want to go. But this isn't the place."

"St. Louis? I'll be going there. You can ride with me."

"St. Louis is fine with me. I can find work there."

"Then St. Louis it will be."

A bugle began blaring. Both Elvira and Fargo noticed a few notes were off-key. She looked at him and chuckled. "Gomer didn't get a wink of sleep all night."

Cooks put out pans filled with scrambled eggs, bacon and ham, gravy, and hot biscuits. Fargo and Elvira were the first in the chow line. As the troopers filed in, Elvira became the center of attention. She rose to the occasion, laughing and flirting with the men, popping her suspenders, making them momentarily forget the bleakness of army life. The troopers appreciated Elvira's antics. Fargo believed they saw in her their wives, daughters, or sweethearts back home.

The room quietened when Fargo and Elvira rose and started for the front door. A soldier stood and began to slowly, evenly stomp one booted foot on the wooden floor. The sound echoed in the otherwise silent room. Another soldier stood, and he, too, stomped in cadence with the first one. Then they all rose to keep the beat. In their own way they were applauding Elvira, not for what she did or didn't do during the night, but because she had captured their hearts. Elvira paused in the doorway, turned to face the crowd, and blew several kisses. The applause was spontaneous and loud.

Fargo led her across the parade grounds to a bench outside the headquarters building, where they sat to talk while watching a spectacular sunrise.

Soon Sergeant Brice came out of the building. He acknowledged their presence with a curt nod, adjusted his cap, then strode onto the parade grounds.

Gomer blew his bugle. All troopers and officers assembled on the parade grounds. Ranks were quickly formed. On command, the soldiers stood at attention. Fargo rose and gestured for Elvira to stand also. With the first note blown by Gomer, the soldiers presented arms and Fargo removed his hat and held it over his heart while observing the posting of the colors. Afterward he and Elvira sat and listened to roll calls, followed by orders for the day, and then "dismissed" rumbled from rank to rank. The troopers broke ranks and walked off the parade grounds. General McRae and Colonel Seymore headed toward Fargo and Elvira.

Approaching, McRae chuckled. "That's a federal offense, young lady, posing as a bugler without a bugle." He stuck out his hand to Fargo.

Shaking it, Fargo jested, "What is the penalty for high treason, General?"

"Death by hanging? Come inside."

McRae moved behind his desk, Seymore crossed to Sergeant Brice's door. Fargo motioned Elvira to sit in the straight-back. They waited for the general to fire up his first cigar of the day. Then Fargo said, "Miss Blassingame has released me. I'm free to accept your commission."

Through a billow of blue-white cigar smoke, McRae chortled, "Fine, fine. How much? I'll pay any reasonable amount for your services."

Fargo took it easy on him. "Five hundred for expenses should do it. Five hundred more upon return of your daughter. Sound fair and reasonable?"

"No. You will need more expense money. Say seven-fifty. I don't want lack of money resulting in a burden for you. Not when my daughter is concerned. I want my child back."

"Five hundred will do. Now, describe your daughter."

McRae's eyes cut to Elvira. "Like I said, Regina is about her size and build. Regina's strawberry-red hair is longer, much longer than this young lady's. And her eyes are light green. They seem to twinkle when she smiles, which is often."

When McRae paused, Fargo said, "A lot of women fit her description. What about her mannerisms, the way she walks and talks, for example?"

"Regina is a refined, proper young woman." Again McRae glanced at Elvira, as though a comparison was made. "Catherine saw to that. Dimples form in Regina's cheeks when she smiles. And she has her mother's southern accent. As for her vocabulary, Regina would die before profanity escaped her lips. And she walks with her shoulders straight. Glides, you might say, rather than a bouncy walk unrefined women have." Once more his eyes darted to Elvira.

"The tone of her voice?" Fargo asked.

"Low soprano. Clear and mellow, barely above a whisper. Catherine abhorred loud females."

"Is Regina energetic? By that I mean physical."

"Oh, no, she's poised, Mr. Fargo. Poised and proper at all times. Catherine taught her that proper ladies never exerted themselves to the point where even the slightest film of perspiration manifested. And in case you are wondering, Regina is not promiscuous. By that I mean"—McRae looked at Elvira—"she is a virgin, pure as driven snow."

Elvira glanced up. "How do you know that?"

"Because, young lady, Catherine made it her business to know. Catherine told me."

Fargo discreetly interrupted before it could go any

further. "That pretty well covers it, General. If I think of anything else before we leave Fort Laramie, I'll let you know." Fargo took Elvira's elbow.

Standing, McRae questioned, "When do you leave? Is Miss Blassingame going with you?"

"Yes," Fargo answered. "We leave for St. Louis at noon today. We have to go into town to purchase trail clothes for Elvira and dispatch a letter to her folks."

"And I will have the cash waiting for you at that hour, Mr. Fargo," McRae intoned.

Fargo had nothing more to say. He walked Elvira to the stable, saddled the pinto, then rode double into town. He dropped her off at the general store and gave her money to buy boots, socks, Levi's, a hat, shirt, and anything else she wanted, then rode to Rockerby's Saloon.

Inside, he ordered a glass of bourbon and took it to a table, where he sat to ponder his mission. Initially, he changed his mind about going to St. Louis. Memphis is where she disappeared, he told himself. That's where I ought to go. Straight to Memphis. On second thought, he reminded himself, a person's first thought usually proves best. Why St. Louis, Fargo, rather than Memphis? He mentally wrestled with the question, but not for long.

He stared out the window. A stagecoach rumbled to a stop across the street. Fargo was deep in thought, and his fixation on the windowpane let him see a hazy, ill-defined blur. A female stepped out of the stage. She, too, was almost lost in his trancelike stare. She began stretching the kinks out of her body. He noticed that, but didn't pay close attention.

Two riders raced by. They were gone in a wink, but the swift movement broke his stare and he brought the stage into focus. The woman wasn't standing at its door. He knew he had seen her only a second ago. Now she wasn't there. He scanned inside the stage. She hadn't stepped back inside it. He leaned over the table and looked at the riders. They were all but out of his sight. And something was amiss about them.

Leaning farther, Fargo brought the riders into sharp focus. Now he saw it: one of the riders was pulling the woman onto his saddle. She was struggling with him.

Fargo dashed outside, leapt into his saddle, and gave chase. He caught up with them less than a quarter-mile out of town. The man not struggling with the woman—she was putting up a hell of a fight with the other man—drew a revolver and started shooting at Fargo. Fargo swerved left to make it harder for the man to swing his gun hand around and track him. At the same time Fargo drew his Colt and fired. The bullet burst the gunman's head. He fell from the saddle and tumbled into a boulder.

The other rider saw Fargo approaching. At the same time the man pulled iron and tried to shove the woman off the saddle. He got off one shot before she jumped and hit the ground, tumbling head over heels. Fargo fired. Blood gushed from the man's neck. He fell onto the horse's neck, then slid from the saddle, dead when he hit the dirt.

Fargo reined the stallion to a halt, dismounted, and went to see about the woman. She was on her hands and knees, shaking the fuzzies from her brain. Helping her to her feet, he asked, "What was that all about, ma'am?"

Her eyes uncrossed. He watched them bring him into focus. A pretty woman—and shapely—she thanked Fargo, then said, "I told the crazy bastard there was no need to rape me, that I'd give them all the pussy they wanted. Damn, my elbows and knees hurt like hell. Look at them, willya? They're all scraped raw. Damn!" She raised the hem of her dress so Fargo could see.

"You a saloon girl? You talk like one."

"Yeah, I'm a saloon girl. Rotten, no-good bastards. I'm glad you killed them. They are dead, aren't they?"

Fargo nodded. "Deader than Kelsey's nuts. Rockerby's Saloon?"

"Yeah, I just got back from visiting my dying aunt

in Fort Kearney. Did you see them snatch my sorry ass right off the street?"

"Barely. It happened fast." He led her to the Ovaro and put her forward in the saddle.

She teased his crotch with her fleshy butt all the way back to the saloon, where Elvira stood waiting on the porch. Fargo dismounted and lifted the whore from the saddle. In midair, she hugged her arms around his neck and kissed him, openmouthed. When Fargo lowered her feet to the ground, she said, "Thanks again, cowboy. You can have my pussy anytime, day or night. You know where to find me."

Fargo touched the brim of his hat. The saloon girl swung her hips as she stepped around Elvira and entered the saloon.

Elvira cooed, "My, my, that was the wettest kiss I've ever watched. I don't want to know what happened between you two on the trail."

"I shot two men. That's what happened. Turn around so I can see your new clothes."

Elvira set Gomer's garb on the porch, then twirled for Fargo. Everything fit nicely. He pulled the hat down over her eyes. "Come on. We need to dispatch that letter."

The Pony Express and stage line shared the same office space. Inside, Fargo watched Elvira pen a letter to her parents, then wrote one of his own, reiterating that she was all right and that he would see to it that she got settled in St. Louis. The two missives were sealed in the same envelope, the clerk was paid, and they left.

They rode into the fort shortly before noon. A cluster of troopers surrounded a lone rider in front of the headquarters building.

General McRae stood with his feet apart on the porch, looking down on the rider.

The iron giant on wheels stood nearby.

4

Crossing the parade grounds, Fargo saw the rider was Indian. Fargo reined the Ovaro to a halt alongside the knot of men.

"Pony-Runs-Long," Elvira whispered.

The Cheyenne war chief sat tall and straight astride an appaloosa. They had gagged him. His wrists were tied at the small of his back. The rawhide binding was so tight that it had cut into the flesh. Blood covered Pony-Runs-Long's hands and dripped from his fingers. He sat expressionless, staring at McRae.

Colonel Seymore flanked the general. Sergeant Brice stood in the doorway. McRae said to nobody in particular, "Throw this savage in the guardhouse. Lieutenant Ross, come inside and report." He glanced at Fargo. "You might as well hear it, too, Mr. Fargo." McRae turned and stepped inside his office.

Four troopers pulled Pony-Runs-Long from his mount. Fargo lowered Elvira to the ground, then eased off his saddle. They watched the war chief be muscled away.

Elvira said, "I'll go see Gomer and give back his uniform. I don't want to hear what happened." She turned and walked away.

Fargo ground-reined the stallion. He leaned against one edge of the doorway to watch and listen. McRae sat behind his desk, Lieutenant Ross stood ramrod straight facing him. Seymore occupied the straight-back, Brice stood in his doorway.

Ross explained, "From my position at the cannon, I observed Lieutenant Hollowell lying on the ground.

Hostiles swarmed all around him. A sizable force of Cheyenne attacked the encampment about the same time the detachment charged. Our forces were greatly outnumbered. I didn't know if Lieutenant Hollowell had been killed or was wounded and unconscious."

"He survived," McRae muttered dryly. "Continue."

"I told the bugler to sound recall. The detachment disengaged and returned to my position. I figured the two groups of Indians would fight it out. I led the detachment east."

No you didn't, Fargo silently corrected. You led it due north.

"Looking behind, I observed the Cheyenne disengaging to the northwest."

Wrong again, Fargo silently mused. They moved due west.

"About two hours before sunset," Ross continued, "Corporal Troutman, riding point, spotted hostiles moving parallel to our column about a mile away. Troutman reported counting nineteen hostiles, all mounted. This matched the detachment's strength. I formed my men into a battle line and had the cannon brought from the rear to the middle of the line.

"The hostiles saw us. Screaming loudly, they charged. The first cannonball hit in the center of the pack of hostiles, killing or wounding a third of them instantly. I ordered my men to move forward at a hard run.

"The surviving hostiles retreated and scattered in hills to the west. I halted my force at the place where the cannonball hit and exploded. The savage wearing this"—Ross paused, held up Pony-Runs-Long's war bonnet for everyone to see—"staggered, apparently in a daze, among the dead and dying. Figuring he was their leader, I took him prisoner. I ordered all the others, dead or wounded, shot.

"That night I had the detachment bivouac on top of a hill. At dawn the column headed back to Fort Laramie."

Fargo watched General McRae rub his face. Then

McRae looked at the big man and asked, "Do we have the Cheyenne war chief, Mr. Fargo?"

"You have him," Fargo answered from the doorway. Moving to stand in the center of the room, he added, "But not for long."

"Oh?" McRae questioned, his brow furrowing.

Fargo explained, "I've seen your guardhouse. Anyone with an ounce of strength could bust out of it. Lieutenant Ross should have killed him when he had the chance."

"Brice," McRae yelled.

"Right here, sir," Brice replied.

"You heard it," McRae began. "Get over to the guardhouse and warn those on duty to keep close watch on the red prisoner. We will hang the son of a bitch at dawn."

As he spoke, gunfire erupted. It came from the general direction of the guardhouse.

"Too late, General," Fargo said wryly. "Pony-Runs-Long is out and running."

McRae shot an order to Colonel Seymore. "Get Gatewood. Tell him I said to take as many men as he needs. I want Gatewood to kill that son of a bitch on sight."

The room cleared. Fargo stepped to the straight-back and sat. He said, "It's time Miss Blassingame and I left, General."

McRae opened the middle drawer of his desk and brought out Fargo's expense money. Handing the bills to Fargo, the general asked, "What's your plan?"

Tucking the money in his hip pocket, Fargo answered, "I will wait for the *Gypsy Queen* to dock at St. Louis. I want to talk to her captain and hear what he has to say about your daughter's disappearance."

"I've already told you Fogg doesn't know anything."

"Yes, you have. Nevertheless, I'll start with Fogg." Fargo stood and offered his hand to McRae, saying, "Don't worry, General. I will bring her back."

McRae shook Fargo's hand, then walked outside

with him. They found Elvira sitting on the porch bench, her hands folded in her lap.

Fargo looked at her and nodded toward the appaloosa. "Think you can handle a war pony?"

"After all I have been through, yes, I can handle anything."

"Then hop on him and we'll be off."

Fargo mounted up. Looking at McRae, he touched the brim of his hat and said, "General?"

"Good luck, Mr. Fargo."

Fargo and the shapely blonde rode across the parade grounds, through the fort's main gate, and headed east, out of Laramie. They had gone slightly less than two miles when Fargo noticed turkey buzzards circling overhead in the distance up ahead. Coming closer, he saw several on the ground stripping flesh off what appeared to be a man's body.

Arriving at the site, Fargo dismounted. The stench overpowered him. He drew his neckerchief up over his nose. Elvira backed the appaloosa upwind, away from the foul odor. As Fargo stepped to the corpse, the buzzards hopped clear of it, but not very far. They watched the big man roll the body faceup with his right foot. Elvira gasped.

It was Lieutenant Maxwell Hollowell. What was left of him. Somebody had taken his tunic. The buzzards had taken his eyeballs and most of his back. Death had come quick to the lieutenant. His throat had been slashed. He had also lost his scalp. Fargo saw three sets of hoofprints, two shod. They had come from the west. After killing Hollowell, the riders had headed north.

"We have to take him back to the fort," Fargo told Elvira. "Get down. I'll put him on your pony."

Elvira dropped to the ground, stepped to the Ovaro, and got into the saddle. She watched Fargo drape Hollowell's body belly-down over the appaloosa's back, then come and get his throwing rope. Minutes later they headed for the fort, trailing the Indian war pony at a good distance.

Elvira mused aloud, "Pony-Runs-Long?"

"Who else? One of the Cheyenne warriors came to his rescue."

"They should have shot the bastard. He's mean. No . . . vicious. I was never so terrified in all my life as I was when he had me. Thank God the Miniconju came and saved me."

He felt her shudder. "Elvira, that's all in the past."

In a hollow voice, Elvira continued to reflect. "They raped me many times, beat me constantly. I was unconscious most of the time. The sorry bastards wouldn't leave me alone. I begged Pony-Runs-Long to kill me. He laughed. They all laughed. I prayed for God to take mercy on me, strike me dead. But he didn't. He saved me, for what purpose I do not know. I think God is punishing me."

Fargo knew her memories of the ordeal would be etched in her mind forever. In time they would fade, but not disappear altogether. He muttered philosophically, "Elvira, what doesn't kill you makes you stronger. Oddly, you are better off from the experience. You suffered and survived. Now you know if it ever happens again, you can live through it."

"Heaven forbid," she replied dryly.

Fort Laramie soon came into view. They entered on the main street. People came out of shops and Rockerby's Saloon to watch their passage. Two young boys ran to get a closer look at Hollowell's corpse. One shouted, "Gollee, he's been scalped clean as a whistle."

The lad's mother hollered, "Sam Unger, you get back on this porch instantly. Hear me, Sam?"

But the boys continued to follow all the way to the fort's main gate. Troopers paused from their work on the parade grounds to watch the couple riding double on the powerful black-and-white pinto stallion, and the half-naked officer's body being trailed behind him. A private grooming a horse near the headquarters building saw the riders coming toward it. He ran to the front door to alert General McRae.

McRae stepped outside as Fargo reined the Ovaro to a halt. Lowering Elvira to the ground, he said. "Lieutenant Hollowell, General."

McRae shouted over his shoulder, "Sergeant Brice! Come out here on the double."

Brice appeared in the doorway behind him. "Sir?"

"Arrange for Lieutenant Hollowell's burial."

Fargo added, "Then give the appaloosa a good bath and bring it back."

Brice winced from the smell when he released the trailing rope.

Fargo dismounted and began coiling the rope. Hanging it on his saddle, he suggested, "The Cheyenne war chief killed him."

"Figures," McRae muttered. "Come in and I'll tell you what happened."

"I'll wait for you here on the porch bench," Elvira said.

"Suit yourself," Fargo replied, and followed the general inside.

McRae spoke as he crossed to his desk and sat. "The shots we heard earlier were fired by an Indian who apparently followed Lieutenant Ross's party back to the fort. He killed the two guards. Hollowell was there. For what reason, nobody knows. They took him hostage, then made their escape. They stole two army horses hitched out front, one for Hollowell to ride and one for the Cheyenne war chief. Major Gatewood and a seven-man patrol left immediately to give pursuit. Now you know what I know. I should've taken your advice, Mr. Fargo, and hanged him immediately."

"Yes, well, Gatewood is an experienced officer. He will run the war chief to the ground. Which way did he go?"

"The two hostiles took Hollowell west. But you—"

"That's right, General," Fargo said when McRae clipped his sentence. "Pony-Runs-Long back-tracked east. I told you the man is cunning. By now he's probably lost to you in the Black Hills."

"Son of a bitch," McRae lamented. "You're right

again, Mr. Fargo. My orders are to stay clear of the Black Hills. Damnation!"

"When the major returns, my advice is for him to start rallying the Lakota. Sooner or later the war chief will break out of the Black Hills. Then he will ride west to fetch as many Cheyenne warriors as he can, and pick up where he left off. He will have to pass through Lakota territory to do it. That's why I say it is urgent that Major Gatewood make friendly contact with the Lakota people."

McRae slammed a fist on the desktop. "I'll do it the moment he returns," he bellowed emphatically.

Fargo could think of nothing more to say. He moved into the doorway and looked at Elvira. The gleaming, dripping-wet appaloosa stood next to his stallion. "Are you ready to ride?" he asked her.

"Yes," she snapped bitterly. "I want the hell out of this place, off the frontier as fast as possible. There is nothing, absolutely nothing out here but grief." She sprung from the bench, strode to the war pony, hiked her right leg, and leapt astride him.

Fargo turned to face McRae. "If there is nothing more, then we'll be leaving."

"You have done more than enough, Mr. Fargo. And I appreciate you imparting some of your wisdom to me."

Fargo nodded. He left the man cupping his hands on the sides of his face, went to his horse, and eased into the saddle. Shortly they rode out of Laramie for the second time this day.

Passing the murder site, they saw no buzzards circling overhead. Fargo continued another twenty miles before stopping to make camp for the night. While he hobbled the appaloosa, Elvira made a small fire and got the coffee brewing. When he returned, he removed the saddle and other gear from the Ovaro and set him to graze with the appaloosa. He noticed Elvira had shucked her Levi's and boots to leave only the long shirt to cover her shapely body.

She drew her knees to her bosom and smoothed the

shirttails over her shins as Fargo approached the fire. "The coffee will be ready in a few minutes," she said. "Aren't the stars beautiful?"

Squatting, Fargo looked skyward and nodded. He found the Big Dipper and noted it hung in the ten-o'clock position. He understood that Elvira's comment about the beautiful stars implied that she felt romantically inclined. He waited to make sure.

Finally she looked at him again, smiled, then said, "Yes, Fargo, the preacher's daughter feels naughty tonight." She slowly, teasingly, parted her knees.

The shirttails crept up her shins just as slowly, high enough to let him glimpse her patch of cornsilky pubic hair. Fargo became aroused at once.

Elvira was all business now. She purred, "No sense in me closing the barn door now that all the cows are out. How do you want me?"

"Before or after?" he threw back, just as teasingly.

"If you mean the coffee, then both."

He pulled off his boots, removed his hat and neckerchief. "On your back."

"Legs parted and down, or the knees raised to ride on your waist?"

He pulled off his shirt. "Up on my shoulders."

"Ah, me," she cooed, and drew the shirttails a little higher.

Fargo took off his gun belt and released his belt buckle.

"My, my, but you do have a beautiful body, Fargo. I can hardly wait to feel those muscles pressing on my body . . . and that one inside me."

He noticed her breathing had quickened in anticipation of the great unknown. Fargo pulled off his Levi's. His hard-on poked through the fly of his underwear.

Elvira gasped, "That is a very nice one. I can hardly wait to taste you."

Fargo hooked his thumbs in the waist of his undershorts and slowly drew them down to his knees.

Elvira yanked her shirt off and crawled to him. "May I?" she whispered.

Nodding, he pulled his undershorts off, then reclined. He felt her left hand spread his thighs and start fondling his gonads, the right grasp his towering manhood and stroke once. Fargo felt his foreskin slip down over the blood-swollen head of it.

Massaging his balls, she mewed, "Fargo, I do declare your bag is full. It needs emptying." Her flaxen hair shielded her pretty face as she bent her head and fed his bulbous summit between her eager lips.

He felt her hot, soft tongue lick the peak several times, then stretch down the soft underside of his length and curl partway around. She fed him deeper and deeper into her hot, moist mouth.

The sensual preacher's daughter gurgled her rapture. "I'm in heaven. This is delicious. Umm . . . yes." She gulped, she swallowed until her mouth and throat captured him fully and her tightly drawn lips encircled his base.

Fargo was amazed she could take in all of it. She came up his hard-on slowly, pausing three times to suck hard, as though reluctant to give it up. When she got to the crown, her lips tightened below it and her tongue swirled furiously all over the crown. Squeezing his scrotum, she moaned, "Blow, Fargo. Let it come."

He willed it to not happen. When her head started bobbing, taking long steady strokes, and the hand on his scrotum massaged madly, both trying to encourage and speed the eruption, Fargo grabbed her hair and pulled her head away.

Her lips smacked when they lost his summit. "My word, Fargo, that was good," she whispered breathlessly. "Why did you make me quit?"

He answered by rolling her onto her back. "Now it's my turn, you little spitfire." He started with her right nipple. He rolled it between his teeth several times, then took in the quarter-sized areola from which the tiny pinkish-brown nipple protruded.

Elvira clawed his back, gasping, "Oh, my God . . . oh, my God . . . yes, yes!"

Fargo sucked in a mouthful of the pillowy breast, then set his tongue to working all over it.

She moaned, arched her back, and murmured joyously, "You're setting me on fire. Suck harder. Bite me, Fargo." She was writhing now.

He slid to the left nipple. Her right hand moved to that breast and cupped it, encouraging him to give her even more pleasure. Fargo captured all the breast his mouth could hold, then drew his lips tight and pulled outward.

Elvira trembled. Her fingernails raked his right shoulder. She gasped between clenched teeth, "Aaagh! Oh, my God . . . that feels so wonderful."

He kissed in her cleavage, then down to her navel, where he paused to probe the indented belly button with his tongue, before moving on down. Elvira parted her legs, raised her hips. His probing tongue met her blood-swollen lower lips. He teased along the slippery slit, then penetrated the hot opening and started circling inside.

She shrieked happily, "I'm ready, Fargo. Oh, God, yes, I'm ready." She shuddered.

Fargo mounted the young, buxom blonde. She spread her slender legs even wider. Using both hands, she positioned his throbbing member for penetration. Fargo entered the juicy tunnel slowly. Her knees came up to his waist. Grunting, she bucked upward. He went in half his length. She raised her ankles to ride on his shoulders. Fargo thrust. He went in all the way.

Elvira gasped loudly, "Oh . . . oh . . . yes, yes. Oh, my God!" Her fingernails dug into his hard buttocks.

Fargo started pumping rhythmically. She met his every thrust with a hard, bucking motion. Her breaths came short and quick now. He felt her insteps move onto his nape, the ankles locked to give her added leverage. Her hips started lunging short and fast. She whispered, "Come with me, darling. Please, come with me."

He felt her body quake, her ankles on his nape

tighten, then her contractions begin. She moaned, "Now, darling . . . now."

He flooded the love nook.

Her knees raked his waist as she milked him dry. Breathing hard, she kissed and nibbled his throat and shoulders, ears, eyes, and cheeks. Fargo framed her face in his hands to stop the energetic, passionate female. With her head immobile, she tried licking his right thumb on her cheek. Fargo kissed her, openmouthed. Her gasps came hot and quick as their tongues fought.

Finally Elvira, exhausted, relaxed her body. The knees came down. Fargo softened and slipped out of the slippery sheath. She whispered, "That was so wonderful. From the first moment I saw you, I wondered if you were the man of my dreams. I know I can't hold you, make you mine, and—"

Fargo touched a finger to her lips to hush her. In the stillness of the moment, as her soft hands caressed his muscled back, he listened to the coffeepot boil and the fire gently crackling. Through those sounds came a new one: a footfall so quiet that only the Trailsman's wild-creature hearing could detect it. His gun hand instantly, automatically reached for his holstered Colt, which was lying on the grass by the fire.

A shot rang out.

Elvira screamed.

The bullet thudded into the ground between his gun hand and Colt. Fargo drew the hand back, rolled off Elvira, and met Pony-Runs-Long's gaze. A warrior stepped around his war chief and kicked the gun belt out of Fargo's reach.

Elvira screamed again.

Pony-Runs-Long's bare left foot stepped on her mouth. Looking down at Fargo, he said, "I saw the black-and-white stallion at the Miniconju *tiospaye*. I saw it again at the soldiers' fort. The Trailsman rides that horse. Are you the Trailsman?"

Fargo nodded once, and then only slightly.

"Tell the woman to be quiet or I will take her scalp."

Fargo repeated him.

Pony-Runs-Long took his foot away.

During the moment, Fargo glanced at his sheathed Arkansas toothpick an arm's length away, lying on the grass behind and between the war chief's feet. The man had stepped right over it.

"Stand up, Trailsman. You are going to lead us in, then out of the Black Hills. Crow Wolf, get my pony."

Fargo's eyes focused on the cylinder of the Smith & Wesson aimed between them. He saw empty chambers only. Either the gun had one bullet in position to fire or it did not. Fargo took the chance it did not. His left hand shot between Pony-Runs-Long's feet and grabbed the stiletto's handle.

Pony-Runs-Long twisted left. The hammer fell. The weapon fired. The slug missed Fargo's left ear by an inch.

The calf sheath and stiletto separated as Fargo raised onto his knees. He threw the knife at the shocked warrior. It buried hilt-deep in the redman's heart. Crow Wolf fell backward, onto the fire, without disturbing the boiling coffeepot.

The war chief pulled the Smith & Wesson's trigger twice in rapid succession. Both times the hammer fell on spent cartridges. Angrily, he threw the useless revolver aside.

Fargo dived and tackled him around the waist.

They tumbled on the ground, rolled, and wrestled to get the upper hand.

Fargo jabbed Pony-Runs-Long in the right kidney. Absorbing the hard blow, the Cheyenne seized his adversary's throat and choked him.

Simultaneously, Fargo slammed his right fist against one side of the war chief's head and his left fist against the other side. Dazed, the Cheyenne chieftain relaxed his grip on Fargo's throat. Fargo powered a right to the man's solar plexus. The war chief grunted and tightened his grip on Fargo's throat.

Again, Fargo pounded the man's head. Pony-Runs-Long's grip tightened even more. The big man wondered what kept him conscious. Fargo's pounding on the war chief's head became increasingly weaker. His senses began fading. Pony-Runs-Long was snuffing out his life.

Pony-Runs-Long came to his knees to finish off Fargo. He snarled, "Die, white man."

Through the buzzing in his ears, Fargo heard his Sharps bark. Relief came instantly from the war chief's stranglehold. Fargo felt the man's weight crash against his body, then warm blood on his left shoulder. Shoving Pony-Runs-Long's body off him, Fargo brought Elvira into focus, and the wisp of gunsmoke escaping the Sharp's barrel.

Slowly, she lowered the rifle and said, "I was afraid to shoot until he knelt."

"You did right, girl," Fargo offered. "The bastard nearly had me."

"I tired you out, sapped all your strength," she claimed in an apologetic tone of voice. "Darling, I'm so sorry."

Fargo started to tell her he could screw all night and still have the strength to whip six big men, which was a fact. Instead he said, "Pour me a cup of coffee." He got up and pulled Crow Wolf's seared body from the fire, then withdrew and wiped the stiletto's blade clean on the dead man's long braided hair.

Elvira handed him a tin cup of the steaming brew. He had taken only two sips when he heard many hoofbeats galloping toward the fire. "Get dressed," he told her. "Company is coming." He reached for his shorts.

They were dressed and standing by the time the riders arrived and reined to a halt at the edge of the firelight.

Major Gatewood looked at the two corpses, then at Fargo, and asked, "The Cheyenne war chief?"

"Get off that army horse, Major, and sit for a spell."

Fargo glanced at and nodded toward Elvira. Through

an easy grin he said, "Miss Blassingame will tell you what happened."

Major Gatewood and his party dismounted and congregated around the small fire. Gatewood looked questioningly at Elvira.

She shook her head and suggested, "Let Fargo explain. It happened so fast that I'm not so sure I remember."

Fargo told them about the two Cheyenne's nocturnal visit, which resulted in their deaths. "Miss Blassingame blew a nasty hole in the war chief's head," he said in conclusion.

Gatewood explained that he and his men were camped in a ravine north of them. A series of knolls prevented them seeing the small fire's glow, but they had heard the shots and Elvira's screams. "We dressed and rushed to give assistance to a female in distress. With your approval, we will make camp here for the rest of the night."

"Fine with me," Fargo replied.

When he looked at Elvira and raised an eyebrow, she nodded.

Gatewood told his men to drag the corpses out of smelling range. "The buzzards can have them," he said.

Fargo handed him a cup of coffee.

5

About three weeks later, Fargo saw a column of jet-black smoke billowing on the eastern horizon. He wondered if luck was with him. Had the smoke been from *Gypsy Queen*? Fargo certainly hoped so.

An hour later the skyline of St. Louis came into view. Several more black clouds of smoke belched skyward, caught in the wind current, and spread rapidly east. A cacophony of whistles signaled the departure of several steamboats. Within a half-hour Fargo and Elvira stood on the west bank of the great river, waiting for a ferry boat to take them to the other side.

Traffic on the river was heavy. Ferry boats came and went across the river in several places. Keelboats caught the flow and headed downstream. Stern-wheelers and side-wheelers, their steam engines set to idle, waited in midstream for berthing alongside a wharf. Those going upstream would berth on the east bank, those heading downstream on the west bank. All had their bows to the current, barely moving, if at all. Steamboats large and small were docked end to end on both sides of the mighty Mississippi. Fancy dressed women holding parasols and men wearing beaver or top hats lined the rails on the vessels' boiler decks. They watched the comings and goings of roustabouts either bringing cargo aboard or off-loading it on the main deck. Poorer passengers stood at rails on the main deck, staying out of the way of the roustabouts and laborers. Bells rang, whistles tooted, smoke poured out the tall, twin smokestacks, most having flared tops to quickly spread the thick smoke and sparks and keep them from falling on the passengers and the steamboat itself. Fargo didn't see the *Gypsy Queen*.

The ferry came and took them to the east bank. Mounting up, Fargo told Elvira, "The *Gypsy Queen* isn't here. We will go into town and buy you some fancy clothes. You want to look nice when inquiring about a job."

Sighing, Elvira nodded.

Fargo watched her halfheartedly attempt to get astride the appaloosa. Usually, she jumped belly-down across the stallion's back, swung her right leg up and over, and raised into a sitting position at the same time. Of late, however, she bypassed all that and simply sprang and rolled to end up astride the horse. Now she did neither. "What's wrong, Elvira? Something bothering you?"

She turned and put her back against the horse's left side. The muscles in her face were tense when she looked up at him and said, "Fargo, now that I'm here, I don't want to stay in St. Louis."

"Oh? Then where do you want to go?"

"I've been thinking about just that for the last two days. I want to go back to Atlanta. Home, Fargo, where I have friends. St. Louis isn't right for me. I'd never find good employment. All I know how to do is play a church piano."

Fargo realized she was homesick. "All right, then, Atlanta it will be. You can ride the *Gypsy Queen* with me to Memphis. A train or stage can take you from there to Atlanta. Are you happy now?"

Pressing her left cheek to his thigh, she reached up and hugged his waist. "Oh, yes, Fargo," she whispered. "I'm so happy."

He felt dampness of her tears seeping through his Levi's pant leg. Ruffling her blond hair, he said, "Here now. Enough of that. Get on that pretty horse and I'll take you to town. We still have to buy the fancy clothes." Elvira kissed the wet spot her tears made, pulled back, and wiped her eyes. He saw she was smiling now. "First, we'll ask around to learn when the *Gypsy Queen* might arrive."

She nodded, then leapt and rolled astride her stallion.

After inquiring about the steamboat three times, and getting "don't know" answers from as many men, the fourth fellow pointed to an open warehouse and suggested Fargo check with the clerk.

They dismounted, walked their mounts to the warehouse, and hitched them to posts holding up the roof. The warehouse was huge in all respects. Bales of cotton were stacked ten high at the far end. Crates, various pieces of machinery, and sacks of grain and rice were piled high and filled the rest of the warehouse. Extremely narrow aisles separated the merchandise. Fargo didn't see anyone who looked official. He stopped two laborers manhandling a heavy box and asked where to find the clerk.

One told him, "Down that way," and nodded in the opposite direction.

Fargo and Elvira started squeezing their way through the tight labyrinth of passageways. Finally they found the bespectacled clerk sitting on a bag of rice, wiping sweat off his neck with a handkerchief. Approaching the haggard young man, Fargo asked him, "You run this place?"

The fellow removed his eyeglasses before answering in a tired voice. "Mr. Abel owns and runs it. I work for Mr. Abel. He's in town on business. What can I do for you?" He started wiping the lenses with the soggy handkerchief.

"A fellow told us you might know when the *Gypsy Queen* is due to arrive."

"Cap'n Fogg took her upriver to Minneapolis. Full load of grain and more immigrants than you can shake a stick at. She's due back in St. Louis two days from now. More or less, depending on whether or not the river is to the liking of her pilot."

"Do you think or know if Fogg will have room for us and our horses?"

"Cap'n Fogg," the clerk corrected. "Don't rightly know. The *Gypsy Queen* is a mighty popular flash packet. I suppose there will be space for the two of you on the main deck. Folks from plantations and businessmen snap up the cabins on her boiler deck first thing." The clerk put his eyeglasses on and then scanned Fargo and Elvira's clothes.

Fargo knew what the clerk was thinking from the way he looked at their attire. The clerk may as well as said they were too poor to afford anywhere other than on the main deck. Touching the brim of his hat, Fargo said, "We have money. Thank you for your time." He gestured for Elvira to precede him through the maze.

At their horses, Elvira volunteered, "My parents and I rode on a steamboat from New Orleans to here. We slept on the main deck. I was never so frightened in all my life. Those men were a rowdy lot. They fought among themselves all the time. Got drunk, too, and stayed that way. More than once I had to fight them off me. The engine noise down there is awfully loud also. So loud one can't think much less sleep. And you have to sleep on the deck. No privacy at all, Fargo."

What she was telling him was that she dreaded the thought of being confined to the main deck. Mounting, Fargo said, "Not to worry, Elvira. You've got me to look after you."

Nothing more was said until they were on a riverfront street lined with saloons and shops of every description. Pedestrians, obviously rich by the clothes they wore, and the not so rich, just as obvious by theirs, mingled as they crossed back and forth to the saloons and shops. The traffic was as thick and busy here as on the river. Piano music flooded out of the saloons. Boisterous male voices spilled out the saloon doors onto the street. Nobody paid any attention to it. Elvira nodded toward a dress shop. Fargo angled for it.

They hitched their stallions to rails out front. Fargo

counted off an even hundred dollars of the expense money McRae had given him, handed it to Elvira, and said, "Going inside dress shops makes me uncomfortable. Buy what you want. I'll be in the Red Rooster Saloon next door. When you're finished, come and stand by the saloon window. I'll watch for you, then I'll come out and take you to that hotel over there." He pointed to a two-story building across the street.

Elvira giggled. "You men," she gently admonished. "You are all alike. You dress us women in fine clothes just to make us take them off. Go to the saloon, Fargo. I'll be out in a minute or so."

He opened the shop's door for her, then went to Red Rooster's swinging doors. As always, Fargo peered inside before stepping in. The saloon was packed. Men lined the long bar. Two fistfights were in progress, one between two rough-cut men pounding hell out of each other between the bar and a row of tables, the other near the piano across the room. Nobody paid any attention to the slug fests. Least of all the saloon girls plying their trade.

A dense haze of blue-white smoke made it near impossible for Fargo to see the far end of the bar. He didn't want to go there, anyhow. He preferred a table by the windows. All but one were surrounded by men playing poker or drinking. That one was occupied by only two men. From their black uniforms and brass buttons, Fargo presumed the pair were steamboat officers. He pushed inside and stepped to their table.

They glanced up from their mugs of beer. Fargo shot them a smile, then asked, "May I join you two gents? I'm waiting for a woman."

"You won't have to wait long," the heavyset one suggested. The other gestured Fargo to sit.

Sitting to face the window, Fargo said, "My name is Skye Fargo." Nodding at the windowpane, he explained, "The woman I'm waiting for is in the dress shop next door."

The heavyset man said, "I'm Captain Moore, and this here is Captain Tanner."

Handshakes were exchanged, then Tanner said, "Captain Moore commands the *Billie Jo* out of New Orleans. I'm the owner of the fastest stern-wheeler on the Mississippi, *Dulce Girl* out of Natchez. How sweet she is." Bouncing his eyebrows, Tanner threw Moore a grin.

Fargo suspected friendly rivalry existed between the two captains. He volunteered that he had noticed Tanner's boat docked on the west bank, then explained, "We are waiting for the *Gypsy Queen* to dock."

"Why wait for Captain Fogg?" Moore intoned. "I leave at daybreak. Where're you going downriver?"

"Memphis," Fargo answered. He quickly added, "A young woman disappeared there. I hold a commission to find her. She was on the *Gypsy Queen*."

Moore and Tanner exchanged serious glances. Moore explained, "Captain Fogg has had four blond passengers disappear in Memphis. All had booked passage to New Orleans. And two now vanished off the *Dulce Girl*, also at Memphis."

"The law couldn't find them," Tanner began. "So what leads you to believe you can?"

Fargo focused on Tanner, "Some folks call me the Trailsman. I'm pretty damned good when it comes to tracking down people. I thought Miss Regina McRae was an isolated case. Now I know differently . . . that many females disappearing at the same place. Tell me about the two you lost, Captain Tanner."

Tanner studied the ceiling while he thought. Finally, he looked at Fargo and began, "Miss Penelope Suddeth was the first to disappear off my steamboat or Captain Fogg's. That was last December. Around Christmastime, wasn't it, Captain Moore?"

Moore nodded.

Tanner continued. "Then the *Gypsy Queen* lost one about a month later. Miss Velma Thackery, one of Joe Thackery's lovely daughters—Joe has a cotton plantation in Mississippi—turned up missing from my *Dulce Girl* within the month. After her, Captain Fogg

72

lost the other three, in as many months, give or take a couple weeks either way."

Fargo claimed, "They are all together. Find one, find all. I'll bet my life on it. How did they disappear?"

Moore's brow furrowed as he asked, "You want to explain that question, Mr. Fargo?"

"By that I mean, what time of the day or night? Did they take their clothing? And were all unattached females traveling alone? I'm seeking commonalities, gentlemen. This many women vanishing into thin air has the smell of their being taken against their will by a person or persons unknown."

Again Tanner looked to the ceiling for answers. He said, "I don't know about the ones aboard the *Gypsy Queen*, but like I've already mentioned, the two from my vessel were not married. Both were young belles, had nice figures, now that I think on it, and they were picture-pretty."

"Go on," Fargo said when Tanner paused. "Day or night?"

"Don't know. Both times we made Memphis around midnight. Didn't miss them till departure time, around noon. Neither female graced a breakfast table that morning. Now, as you will see, Mr. Fargo, missing breakfast when in port isn't uncommon at all. Especially in regard to the ladies. First-class passengers hold first-class tickets and often go shopping in town. So nobody so much as raised an eyebrow when the young ladies didn't appear for breakfast.

"I always watch for my first-class passengers to return. When departure time drew near and neither had returned, I sent the second mate to look for them. He reported not finding them on deck or in the ladies' cabin. I personally went and knocked on their doors. Their doors were not locked, Mr. Fargo. After calling their names several times, I stepped inside. In both instances the beds had been slept in. The dresses I had seen them wearing the evening before were draped on the chair. A search of the closet was made. No clothing appeared to be missing. I wanted to make sure.

So I asked an older woman to look. Both times the older woman said the same thing."

Moore's curiosity to know "the same thing" was a tad stronger than Fargo's. Moore blurted, "What?"

Fargo believed he knew the answer. He said, "Not one stitch of clothing was missing. Both ladies were naked when they disappeared."

"That's right, Mr. Fargo," Tanner mused. "Completely and totally naked."

"Did you report this to the sheriff?" Fargo asked.

"Certainly. The lawmen were as baffled as anyone else. How could a nude young woman get off the boat without anyone seeing her? My God, man, there's more than a hundred people on the main deck. She would have had to walk through that mob to get to the wharf."

"What did the law conclude?"

Moore answered, "The obvious. They committed suicide by jumping overboard during the night."

"I think not," Fargo muttered dryly. In a stronger voice he continued, "An interesting mystery, gentlemen. Like I've said, find one, find all. The question becomes: in which direction were they taken?"

"And by whom?" Tanner quickly added.

As Fargo and Moore nodded solemnly, a buxom saloon girl came up behind Fargo. Feeling his right bicep, she whispered in his left ear, "I bet the muscle hanging between your legs is bigger'n this one. Want me to massage it in my tender place?"

Fargo chuckled. "No. These gentlemen and I are talking business. Why don't you bring me a beer? Give the captains a refill."

Rebuked, she grabbed the empty beer mugs and strode to the bar. She reappeared momentarily, flanked by three tough-looking men. One had a weal that ran from his forehead, through his left eyebrow, jumped over the eyeball, then carved straight down his left cheek. Another hadn't been so lucky: he wore a black patch over the missing right eyeball. The third, younger than the other two and more muscular than either of them, showed no battle scars. He wore a much-abused beaver hat cocked jauntily on fiery-red hair.

Patch growled, "Big man, Missy Delores says you offended her. I say apologize to her."

Fighting words, Fargo thought as he and the two steamboat captains stood and pushed their chairs back.

The trio of toughs assumed fighting stances. All three balled their hands into fists. Now Fargo saw Beaver Hat's battle scars. They were limited to his knuckles. As Fargo grinned and stared at the black patch, he calmly cracked his knuckles and said, "Stand back, captains. I think these river rats are spoiling for a fight."

Patch dived over the table.

Fargo's right fist slammed into Patch's jaw while he was in midair. Patch groaned as he fell off the tabletop.

Weal lunged at Fargo. Sidestepping him, Fargo laid an uppercut into Weal's mouth and nose. The hard blow split Weal's lips, broke his nose. He tumbled into Captain Moore's chair.

Now it was Beaver Hat's turn to test Fargo's mettle. The man commenced dodging and ducking. Fargo waited too long for an opening. The youngster's left hand shot out lightning-fast and struck Fargo's head.

Fargo reeled from the powerful blow. His ears rang and his eyes crossed. He shook his head to clear his brain of the swirling purple stars.

Beaver Hat laughed as he hit Fargo again, this time a solid right to the abdomen.

Fargo's face crunched against the tabletop. He gasped for air.

Fists pummeled his head, back, and kidneys, too many for only one man to throw. Although dazed and hurting, Fargo sensed the trio had collected behind him to polish him off. He mustered the strength to stretch his leaden arms out over the tabletop. Then he flopped over and closed his arms around the threesome.

Caught by surprise, they quit pounding Fargo to wrench free of his tight arm grip. That was a mistake, for the error in judgment gave Fargo time to clear his head. He needed fighting room.

The Trailsman eyed the front window. Tightening his grip on them, he muscled all three toward the window as fast as he could, and with a snarling growl he hurled himself and the three men through the window, tumbling onto the porch.

Fargo sprang to his feet and pulled Beaver Hat erect. He drove a hard right to the youngster's jaw. The jab not only broke the jawbone, it also opened a wound in Beaver Hat's chin, a wound that would leave a scar. Beaver Hat grunted and fell unconscious onto the porch.

Patch and Weal had made it to their hands and knees. Fargo grabbed two fistfulls of their hair, then rammed their heads together. Both sank to the porch, unconscious before they hit it facedown.

The two steamboat captains applauded from where they stood near the shattered window.

Elvira's voice said, "Let you out of my sight for one minute and you get into a fight. Fargo, I don't know what I would do without you around to protect me."

He looked at her as he sucked the scraped spots on his right knuckles. He saw her arms laden with cute boxes small and large. Relieving her of them, he suggested they proceed to the hotel.

Inside, the desk clerk told Fargo there were no vacancies on the lower floor. "I have two rooms upstairs. Both overlook the river."

"We'll take one," Elvira replied.

The clerk handed her the key to Room 9.

In the room, Fargo dumped the boxes onto the bed, then stepped to the window, parted the curtains, and tugged the window open. He stood there a moment or two, listening to and watching the traffic on the river. When he turned, Elvira lay naked among the boxes.

She smiled naughtily and reminded him, "You promised that next time you'd show me how Apaches do it. I'm ready to learn."

Fargo sailed his hat into a corner of the room. "A promise is a promise," he told her. Next, his neckerchief fluttered to the floor. "And I always keep my promises." He removed his gun belt and laid it in the chair. "Plaster your back against any wall."

"Oh, goody," the shapely preacher's daughter chortled as she quickly left the bed to obey.

Afterward they put the boxes on the floor and sprawled on the bed to relax. Fargo suggested they nap until sundown.

"What happens then?" Elvira asked. "Apache style again? It was thrilling for me."

"No, Elvira. After the nap, we go bathe, then eat the biggest steaks in town."

"Then we will—"

"I'm not making anymore promises to you," Fargo hurried to say. He was ready to believe all the woman had on her mind was crawling in bed with him.

"Aw," she jokingly pouted. "I done gone and plumb tuckered my big darling."

He gave her an intimidating look, one that clearly conveyed "don't say anything like that anymore." Fargo put her head in the crook of his left shoulder. They drifted into sleep listening to the sounds of the city and river.

The evening sun set half down on the horizon when Fargo awakened Elvira. They dressed, then went down to bathe. There was no problem for Fargo finding a place to have a bath; the barber shop across the street and down a ways advertised "nickel tubs of hot Mississippi water."

Elvira asked, "What about me?"

"Not to worry, woman." He took her arm and led her to a two-story house on the next street.

A jolly black woman wearing a white, starched

77

maid's uniform answered the door. She flung the screen door open, seized Fargo in a bear hug, and shrieked, "Lawdy, lawdy, big'un, you sure 'nuff feel good!" Over her shoulders, she hollered, "Miss Holly, Miss Holly! Come quick an see who I catched. Lawdy, lawdy, goodness, gracious, sake's alive, big'un, you're a sight for sore eyes." She lightened her embrace.

Helplessly, Fargo muttered, "Elvira, this is Claudine Monroe. Let go, Claudine, before you bust my ribs."

Claudine released him just as a tall redheaded woman stepped to the doorway. The redhead had broad hips, big breasts, and too much rouge on her cheeks. Her clear light-green eyes shone as she smiled and said, "Well, I do declare, look what the cat drug in. Hello, Fargo. Long time no see. I was beginning to think Indians had scalped you. Come here. I want to hug and kiss you." She opened her arms.

Fargo stepped into them. Embracing him, she raised on tiptoes and kissed him, openmouthed. A soft blush appeared on his face. He broke the kiss and muttered, "Elvira, meet Holly Chastain, the absolute best working woman in town."

Miss Holly reached around the big man and shook hands with Elvira.

Claudine suggested everyone step inside before a crowd collected on the street. "That old prune-face biddy will show up sure as hell," Claudine offered.

Inside the spacious parlor three other women lounged on sofas. All shot Fargo winsome smiles.

A husky, bald, jet-black man stood behind a small bar. When he smiled at Fargo, two gold upper front teeth gleamed.

Fargo said, "Hello, Tucker. How about pouring me a shot of bourbon?"

"Coming right up, Mr. Fargo," Tucker replied in a deep bass voice.

Elvira crossed to Miss Holly's grand piano. She admitted, "This is the prettiest piano I ever saw."

"Do you play?" Miss Holly asked. When Elvira

nodded, the buxom madam suggested she sit and try it out.

Fargo moved to stand at the bar and sip his bourbon while listening to Elvira play the piano. Fargo had never heard the piece she played. Apparently nobody else in the room had, either. They sat with trancelike expressions on their faces throughout the haunting, foreboding piece Elvira played.

At the conclusion, Elvira said, "I've not practiced in a long time. That piece was written by Wagner."

"You're hired," Miss Holly said. "I need a touch of class around this house. You're hired," she repeated.

"No she isn't," Fargo replied. "Right now she needs a bath."

Miss Holly snapped her fingers. "Ruth Anne, you and Roxie fill a tub and give her a good scrubbing." Turning to Fargo, she went on, "You can use my private tub."

Elvira followed Ruth Anne and Roxie up the stairs.

Fargo walked with Miss Holly to her downstairs living quarters. Watching her fill the tub, he asked, "Why aren't your girls busy with customers? The last time I was here, you couldn't handle the traffic. What happened?"

"That bible-thumping old biddy Claudine mentioned, that's what happened. The high-toned bitch has run everybody away. Spinster Hattie Baugh stands out front and beats her drum and gives all the men a dose of her hellfire and brimstone. Oh, how I hate that woman. She's ruining my business." Miss Holly shed her clothes.

"Uh, Holly, all I want is the bath."

She looked at him disbelievingly. "The blond piano player? What'shername?"

"Elvira Blassingame."

"You sweet on her?"

He chuckled. "No, I'm not sweet on her. It's just that I know what would happen if I got in your saddle." He put a foot in the water. "Two more buckets of hot water should do it."

"Ain't got no more hot. What would happen?"

Fargo settled down into the tub. Gooseflesh immediately appeared on his arms and chest. He sunk below the surface to get it done and over.

When he came up, Missy Holly questioned, "Well, answer me, Fargo. What would happen?"

"You wouldn't let me loose till midnight."

"So?"

"So, Elvira and I have other plans."

"Just as I thought: you are sweet on her." Miss Holly stood and started getting dressed. Walking out of the room in a made-up huff, she commented, "I'll be in the parlor."

Fifteen minutes later Fargo, refreshed, joined her and Tucker at the bar. "Thanks for the bath, Holly. Next time I'll be more amenable."

A drum started beating. A shrill female voice started singing a hymn Fargo didn't recognize. He moved to the screen door. A tall, thin woman dressed in black stood out front, beating a big drum, screeching the hymn off-key. After a few minutes she stopped singing and walked away banging her drum. Fargo watched her round the corner and head toward the street the hotel was on.

"See what I mean?" the madam said.

Fargo nodded.

Shortly, Elvira, Ruth Ann, and Roxie appeared at the top of the stairs. Elvira called down to Fargo, "I'm spic-and-span clean again." He watched her come to him. "I'm starving, Fargo."

"I am, too." Turning to Miss Holly, he said, "Thanks for the baths. We will be leaving now."

She asked, "When will you be back?"

"Next time," he answered wryly, touched the brim of his hat, and nudged Elvira toward the door.

Outside, they walked with an arm around each other's waist. Going to a café two doors down from the Red Rooster Saloon, they passed in front of a dark opening between the saloon and a steamboat office.

Three men leapt out of the dark and pulled them to the ground.

Elvira screamed.

The men hammered their fists against Fargo's head and body. He doubled up and covered his head and face. The Trailsman heard three sharp whacks. Immediately the fists stopped beating on him. He parted his fingers and saw Beaver Hat sprawled facedown in the dirt, the other two lying at his feet.

"Sonny boy, are you all right?" a whiskey voice asked.

Fargo rolled over and looked up at an older, portly man dressed much like Captains Tanner and Moore. The man rested on a gnarled walking stick. He wasn't smiling. Coming to his feet, Fargo said, "Thanks, friend. Who do I owe this debt to?"

"Captain Fogg."

6

"Captain of the *Gypsy Queen*?" Fargo asked. He pulled Elvira to a sitting position, then cradled her in his arms.

"One and the same, laddie. The girl isn't hurt. Poor woman swooned on sight of these three ruffians. Keel-boaters all, they be."

Fargo patted Elvira's face. "I had a run-in with them earlier at the Red Rooster. How do you know they're keel-boaters?"

"That one doubled up like a baby there is Jeremy Hollister. Those two lying across each other, the one with the knife scar on his face, put there by Big Jim Pennyworth, is Mudcat Johnson. The other answers to Ralph Anders. I haul 'em up to Cairo from Natchez or New Orleans all the time. But they missed getting off at Cairo this time because they were stone-cold drunk. Sobered up by the time the *Gypsy Queen* made it to St. Louis. Said they'd wait for her here. Though they are a tough lot, they aren't killers. The little lady is coming around."

Dazed, Elvira moaned, "What happened?"

"Top o' the evening to you, madam," Fogg said, touching the brim of his hat.

Fargo explained, "Captain Fogg was telling me about these bozos that attacked us."

"Captain Fogg?" She glanced at him.

"At your service, ma'am."

"But, but, I thought the *Gypsy Queen* wasn't due until—"

"My pilot made fast headway," Fogg interrupted.

Looking at Fargo, Fogg continued, "I saw Captain Tanner at the steamboat office. He told me about the fight. Tanner also said you wanted passage on the *Gypsy Queen* to Memphis and why. Go aboard, Mr. Fargo. Tell the chief clerk I said to give you a cabin. We leave in the morning." He nodded to Elvira, then walked to the Red Rooster and went inside.

Fargo stood and pulled Elvira to her feet. He looked at the trio. They were stirring awake, groaning and feeling the knots on their noggins. He took Elvira's arm and led her to the hotel. They collected the boxes and left the room. Just as Fargo handed the clerk the room key, the spinster started beating her drum, screeching a hymn.

The clerk grimaced. Nodding toward the door, he said, "Somebody ought to shut her up. All that racket hurts my ears."

Fargo tossed a grin to the clerk. The big man led Elvira out on the porch. Suddenly, Hattie stopped banging the drum. She screamed, "Give back my drum and bible. Hear me? I said give them back. I mean now!"

Fargo saw the terrible trio had recovered from Fogg's shellacking. They and the high-tone woman were in the street in front of the Red Rooster. The men pitched the drum and big bible back and forth to one another. They thought it was funny to keep them out of reach of the spinster's hands. She was leaping, jumping, trying to grab either of the items, hollering all the time, "You'll be sorry you did this. God will strike all three of you blind. Blind, I say! Blind as He did to Saul of Tarsus on the road to Damascus."

"They're being mean to that poor woman, Fargo," Elvira hissed. "Do something!"

Fargo handed her his load of boxes. He ambled toward the fracas. Mudcat Johnson saw him coming and warned his pals. Jeremy rubbed the knot Fogg's shillelagh had raised on his head, as though the big man approaching put it there and he couldn't figure out how. The spinster yanked her drum from Jeremy's grasp. Mudcat wisely pitched the bible to her. Then the trio fled in the darkness between buildings.

Hattie Baugh smoothed her ankle-length black dress as Fargo walked up to her and asked, "You all right, ma'am?" He touched the brim of his hat.

Flustered, Hattie said, "God will punish them. He will reward you, mister. You are a Good Samaritan."

"Don't know about that, ma'am." He shot her a grin with a wink.

She blinked as she watched him amble to his and Elvira's horses. Fargo lifted Elvira astride the appaloosa, then relieved her of most of the boxes. Mounting up, he noticed Hattie hadn't moved and had a perplexed expression on her gaunt face. Riding past her, he paused, "You sure you're all right, ma'am?"

Hattie nodded. "I'm fine, thank you."

He tipped his hat and rode on.

"That was considerate of you, Fargo," Elvira muttered. "While I don't agree with street preaching—Daddy made Mama and me stand all pious-looking while he preached on the streets of Atlanta—I feel pity for those who do, especially women."

Nothing more was said until they came to the *Gypsy Queen*. The three-decker flash packet was painted white, trimmed in bright red, and had twin black smokestacks that stood tall with crowns fit for a queen gracing their tops. A nice-looking cross brace of black wrought iron connected the smokestacks. On the support were red block letters that spelled the packet's name. A uniformed ship's officer stood on the main deck at the end of the gangway. A lean man, he had a handlebar mustache and held a ledger book.

Fargo called to him, "Are you the chief clerk?"

The fellow nodded.

"Captain Fogg told us to see you about a ticket to Memphis."

The officer gestured them to board.

They dismounted and led their horses across the gangplank. The chief clerk stepped aside. Looking at their clothing—a sure indication of their ability or inability to pay—he said, "That'll be two dollars each. Hitch your horses aft. You'll see where. Then pick a place to sleep. Captain Fogg doesn't tolerate loud singing or too much rowdiness."

Elvira blurted, "I thought the Captain said—"

Fargo hurried to interrupt. Staring into the chief clerk's watery eyes, he told the man, "Captain Fogg said for you to provide us with private quarters."

The clerk's tone of voice was filled with disbelief when he said, "Oh, did he, now? I don't have any vacancies on the boiler deck. Listen, cowboy, I don't want any trouble out of you."

"I'm no cowboy," Fargo snarled.

"He's a trailsman, Mr. Post," Fogg's whiskey voice corrected from the wharf end of the gangplank. He moved midway on the gangplank and said, "Mr. Post, put my guests in Vermont."

Post stammered, "But, but, Captain, Mr. Clark occupies Vermont."

Fogg raised and stared at his chief clerk.

Intimidated, Post mumbled, "Yes, Captain, I'll see that Vermont is made ready." He turned to Fargo. "If you will hitch your horses where I said, then come to the saloon for dinner. I will make the necessary arrangements for your accommodations."

Fargo nodded. He asked Fogg, "Need my help?"

"No, laddie. You two go on. I'll join you at the dinner table."

They found beds of straw in the individual stalls near the stern. Most were empty. They led their mounts into two. While Elvira poured the appaloosa a bucketful of oats, Fargo set the boxes on the deck, then relieved the Ovaro of his burden and fed him oats.

A young black boy—Fargo guessed his age at fifteen—entered the stall area. He exclaimed, "Lordy, lordy, you folks have pretty horses. Yes sir, mighty pretty. My name's Homer, sir. I take care of the horses. Give 'em fresh water, hay, and sing to them at night or when they act skittish. Groom 'em, too . . . for a nickel."

"Clean around their frogs?" Fargo questioned.

"Sure, mister. I do that, too."

"Dress down the saddle and tack?"

"Yes sir. Dressing costs a dime more. I do a good job, though, not a lick an' a promise like those other steamboat stable boys. Cap'n Fogg, he insists on us giving his passengers good service. First-class or main-deck tickets don't make no difference to him. A fare is a fare, he claims."

"Wise man," Fargo muttered. He fished in his pockets for coins. Handing fifty cents to Homer, Fargo said, "Groom them both. Dress all tack, my saddle and stirrups. Wash and dry my saddle blanket. Where do I put my bedroll?"

"I'll see to it," Homer answered.

Fargo draped his saddlebags over one shoulder. Sharps in hand, his arms loaded with boxes, he gestured Elvira to precede him out of the stall area. She went forward, to a semispiral staircase leading up to the gallery on the boiler deck.

Going up the stairs, Elvira whispered, "The captain of the steamboat that took my parents and me to St. Louis wouldn't allow main-deck passengers to set foot on his precious stairs. Fargo, I'm excited." She squeezed his arm.

They stepped onto the gallery. It reminded Fargo of a shade arbor. White railings went around the open front and sides of the gallery, then those on the sides continued all the way aft to the huge paddles. Intricate patterns of gingerbread woodwork were everywhere. Tables and chairs, arranged for first-class ticket-holders, went unoccupied at this hour. A door with a large brass handle stood at the rear of the gallery. Fargo opened the door.

Elvira gasped and raised her hands to her bosom. "Oh, Fargo, it's so beautiful," she said in a hushed, almost reverent tone of voice.

They stood looking down a long hall about ten feet

wide that ran all the way to the *Gypsy Queen*'s stern. Rich, ornate draperies and gleaming mirrors hung on the walls. The many chairs and sofas—all with blood-red cushions—that stood all about the length of the hall captured Fargo's attention. They looked exceedingly comfortable.

Huge, glittering crystal lamps hung in a row from the high ceiling. The arched beams across the ceiling were trimmed with gingerbread painted white and gold. Each end of the curved beams was supported by a gleaming white wooden column. On the other side of the columns, separated by no more than three paces, were the inner doors to the staterooms.

In the front corner to Fargo's right stood the bar, manned by two middle-aged black men. The bar had a shiny brass rail. Its ornately carved woodwork was highly polished and fairly gleamed. Fargo glanced at the shelves behind the bartenders. They were lined with bottles of the finest wines and liquors, a far cry from the red-eye whiskey the big man was used to seeing in the saloons on the frontier.

A ruby-red grand piano awaited a person to play it. The piano stood between two columns near the bar. Fargo noticed a barber shop between two others across the hall from the piano.

Plush, deep-red carpeting covered the floor from wall to wall. Snowy tableclothes covered the long dining tables arranged diagonally for the evening meal. Gleaming silverware and fine china adorned the tables. At one end of each stood a waiter dressed in a starched white uniform.

Most of the diners glanced up from their food and looked at Fargo and Elvira. One of the bartenders approached Fargo. The fellow spoke for all the fancy-attired first-class passengers when he said, "Main-deck passengers aren't permitted in the saloon. You all best leave."

Fingering his beard, Fargo scanned above the crowd's heads, hoping to spot the chief clerk. Not seeing him,

Fargo muttered, "Where does Captain Fogg take his meals?"

The bartender cleared his throat. Fargo heard him snap his fingers, clearly a signal to the other bartender that he faced a belligerent main-deck passenger and needed help in throwing the big man out. As the other bartender moved to comply, the first repeated, "You all best leave."

"Come on, Fargo," Elvira nervously suggested, "before you get into another fight. We'll go find Captain Fogg."

At that precise moment Fogg came through the doorway behind her and Fargo. "Did I hear my name?" He stepped around Fargo, looked at the pair of husky bartenders, and asked, "Rafer, do you and Jeansonne here have a problem with seating my guests?"

Rafer and Jeansonne visibly relaxed. Rafer smiled as he answered, "No, sir, Cap'n, sir. We just thought—"

"You just thought by the way they are dressed they belonged on the main deck."

"Yes, sir."

"Well, you're wrong, Rafer. Where is Mr. Post? I sent him up here to make arrangements for my guests to occupy Vermont."

As he spoke, Fargo saw the chief clerk step from an inner stateroom door near the far end of the great saloon. Fargo nodded in that direction. "I think Mr. Post is coming to tell us now."

"It's about time," Fogg replied. Aiming his noggin-knocker at a table, he continued, "After putting your stuff in your cabin, you will find me at that table." He walked toward the table.

The chief clerk smiled as he approached Fargo. "Vermont is ready. I'll show you the way."

"Not necessary," Fargo grunted. "I saw which door you stepped out of. Follow me, Elvira."

They walked between the support columns and the inside wall decorated with scenes that highlighted historic or famous events that occurred in the states named on the doors. Fargo glimpsed a slave auction when he passed Mississippi, the signing of the Constitution when he walked by Pennsylvania. At Vermont there was a man collecting sap from pails attached to maple trees. He opened the door to Vermont and stepped aside for Elvira to enter first.

Again, she gasped, not from the elegance she saw, but from the stateroom's size: there was barely enough space for one person to move around in, much less two, especially one of Fargo's size. A double-decker bunk formed and filled one wall. A single chair stood against the wall opposite the bed. Above the chair and to the left, a shelf held a washbasin and a pitcher of fresh water. Across from the saloon door was another door and, next to it, a small window covered by a shutter. Elvira opened the door.

Fargo looked over her shoulder. White railings lined the open gallery that ran the full length of the boiler deck.

Elvira mumbled, "Fargo, you will have to stand outside to braid my hair. There's not enough room in here to breathe. I hate those bunks. We will never be able to get into just one. They're not long enough for your length without sleeping with your knees bent. Oh, my, I thought these cabins would be bigger, much bigger." She stepped to the chair and set her boxes on the seat.

Fargo dumped his on the lower bunk. Rubbing his face, he suggested, "We will spend most of our time either outside or in the saloon, anyway. Wash your face, then meet me in the saloon. You'll know where to find me."

Elvira sighed and nodded. Two strides brought Fargo to the door.

He joined Fogg and five others—three men and two matronly appearing older women—seated at the table. A feast fit for a king lay before them: roast duck, roast beef, fried catfish filets, leg of lamb, raw and cooked vegetables the likes of which Fargo had never seen, bowls of gravies . . . it went on and on. As he sat, the waiter filled Fargo's crystal stemmed glass with a French burgundy wine. Fargo carved off a piece of the duck's plump breast.

Captain Fogg opened the conversation from where he sat at one end of the dining table. First, he introduced Fargo and the others. The women took precedence. "Mr. Fargo, the lady on your right is Mrs. Florence Jance. The lovely lady sitting across from her is Mrs. Bellah Farnsworth. Their husbands, George on Florence's right, Philip on Bellah's left, are plantation owners in Louisiana. Sugarcane, best I remember. Right, George?"

"I grow rice and cotton," Jance corrected. "Farnsworth raises cane."

"And hell," mumbled Philip's spouse.

That spawned chuckles from the men.

Fogg continued, "And the fellow sitting at the far end of our table is William Bennett, the only northerner to grace our table other than myself. William is out of Washington, D.C. Probably scouting for the rail-splitter, although he'd never admit it." When Fogg paused, Bennett nodded toward Fargo. Fogg went on, "Mr. Fargo has been commissioned by General Scott McRae to find his daughter, Regina. The lovely young lady disappeared from this steamboat under mysterious circumstances last July."

"Really?" Florence intoned. Glancing up from her fork of roast beef, she asked, "Where did the young woman disappear?"

Fargo answered, "At or near Memphis."

"Don't you know, Captain?" queried Bellah.

"No. Not exactly," Fogg began. "I saw Miss McRae at dinner the night before I docked in Memphis at noon the next day. She vanished sometime between dinner and docking."

Fargo hurried to ask, "How do you know Regina didn't walk off the boat, then disappear in Memphis?"

"Mr. Fargo, I am in the pilothouse every time the *Gypsy Queen* docks at a wharf. From that lofty height, I watch my first-class passengers go ashore, mentally note those who do not. Miss McRae did not go ashore that day."

"Maybe she went ashore after you left the pilothouse," Florence Jance offered. And Fargo silently agreed.

"No, madam, she did not. When I didn't see the young lassie on deck that morning, I sent Mr. Post to look in on her, to see if she was all right. He reported he found her cabin, the Vermont"—Fogg paused to glance at Fargo—"the same cabin you occupy, Mr. Fargo, in great disarray. I asked Mrs. Huckaby to account for Miss McRae's personal belongings. Clothing and such."

"And?" Bellah wondered aloud.

"And nothing was missing. Not a stitch."

Bellah gasped, "That means she disappeared na—"

"Yes," Fogg said. "Completely." He sipped from his wineglass during the ensuing silence.

Fargo could only imagine what was running around inside the heads of those seated at Captain Fogg's table. They were probably having much difficulty reconciling a nude female being on deck without somebody noticing. Therefore, he wasn't surprised to hear Philip Farnsworth suggest, "The young woman in question probably stepped outside, became faint, and fell overboard."

Nodding, Fogg agreed, "That's one possibility, Philip. But I think not. You see, four other young, unattached ladies disappeared under similar circumstances before Regina McRae."

"Four?" gasped Florence and Bellah.

Sniffing the burgundy's bouquet, Fargo said, "Tell me about those disappearances."

Before Fogg could reply, Elvira arrived. She wore one of her new dresses, white satin, the hem of which touched the carpet. She had fixed her hair, too. The blond tresses were gathered behind her head and tied with a big white bow. Ringlets graced her forehead. Elvira smiled winsomely. Every man at the table stood.

Fargo couldn't imagine she was the same woman he had rescued from the Miniconju encampment only a short time ago. She wore a delicate perfume also. Seating her, Fargo said, "This is my assistant, Miss Elvira Blassingame." He went on to introduce the other guests, after which the men sat. Fargo explained to Elvira, "Captain Fogg is about to tell us what he knows about young ladies disappearing off his steamboat. You can listen as you eat. The duck is delicious."

The waiter filled her glass with wine. As he stepped back, Fogg spoke. "A Macon, Georgia, banker's daughter was the first to go. Miss Penelope Suddeth had passage from Cairo to New Orleans. As a matter of fact, all of them held first-class tickets to New Orleans. And all were missing when I docked in Memphis. Miss Suddeth's nightdress was missing. Only the nightdress. So, I and the sheriff presumed she had it on at the time she disappeared."

"When did she disappear?" Bellah inquired.

"All of them were at dinner the evening before the morning the *Gypsy Queen* docked in Memphis. They vanished during the night. What hour, nobody knows."

When Fogg paused and motioned the waiter to give him a refill of the burgundy, Fargo questioned, "Assuming they were physically taken against their will, did passengers in the adjoining cabins say they heard a struggle? The walls *are* thin."

"Not one peep," Fogg answered. He turned to the waiter. "Socrates, fill my glass to the brim."

"Assuming a main-deck passenger took them," Fargo persisted, "do you have any idea who regularly gets off in Memphis?"

Fogg chuckled. "Yes, too many to count. Salesmen, keel-boaters, and the like. As I mentioned, I watch over my first-class passengers. I don't pay any attention to those on the main deck. But the sheriff asked the same question."

Nodding, Fargo implored, "Please continue, Captain. Who was next to vanish?"

"Miss Rebecca Carlisle, a plantation owner's lovely and lively daughter."

"Ben Carlisle has a thousand acres of sugarcane near Baton Rouge," Philip Farnsworth explained. "I didn't know Rebecca had disappeared until now. Did you, Bellah?"

Bellah shook her head. "No, Clara and Ben must be terribly distraught. We must go see them, Philip."

Fargo said, "Tell the Carlisles you met me. Tell them the Trailsman will find their daughter, wherever she is."

Elvira put down her fork, scanned the faces seated around the table, then said, "And I promise Fargo will find her. I'm proof of that. I was captured by a Cheyenne war chief earlier this year. Miniconju Sioux subsequently stole me from the Cheyenne by accident. Fargo found me in the Miniconju *tiospaye*. Later, he killed the war chief. If he found me in all that wilderness, he will surely find Rebecca Carlisle."

They all stared at the big man, as though seeing him for the first time, as though he was a terror on the loose.

Finally, Fogg mused, "Are you an Indian-fighter, Mr. Fargo?"

"No, not really. Most Indians are my friends. I fight only those who test me. War Chief Pony-Runs-Long tested me and died for doing it. By now the buzzards have picked his bones clean."

Bellah gasped. Florence grabbed her mouth, jumped up, pushing her chair over backward, and ran for her stateroom, with Bellah close behind.

The waiter immediately righted the chair and returned it to its place.

"My wife is the squeamish type," George Jance muttered, "but I'm not. Please, Mr. Fargo, continue."

"I was finished," Fargo said. He looked at Captain Fogg, implying he wanted him to pick back up on his story.

Fogg chuckled. "If I had known how handy you are with your fists, I would have waited to see the final outcome of your fight with the keel-boaters. Anyhow, Miss Carlisle disappeared with no clothes on also. So did Miss Frances Anne Budreaux. She is the youngest, eighteen years old, of Jean-Claude and Lolita Budreaux's three daughters. Jean-Claude owns an import-export business in New Orleans.

"The one before Regina McRae was Agatha Marie Deleconte, also eighteen, and the daughter of Frank and Winifred Deleconte. Frank sells slaves at auction in New Orleans. Frank's four boats stay busy bringing slaves from Africa. Agatha Marie's pantaloons disappeared with her." He raised his eyebrows questioningly when he looked at Fargo.

"That makes seven in all, five from the *Gypsy Queen* and two off Captain Tanner's *Dulce Girl*," Fargo began. "They are all together. The question becomes, on which side of the Mississippi?"

"Laddie, it's a big world out there, and most of it is far more dangerous than life on this river. All I can tell you is that law authorities from as far west as Little Rock and east to Nashville were alerted. So far none has reported seeing a collection of young southern belles."

Fargo could believe that. "Money talks. Have reward posters been circulated, nailed to every tree?"

"Certainly," Fogg answered. "Seven thousand dollars for their safe return."

A low whistle escaped Fargo's lips. "God, Captain Fogg, that's more than enough to cause every soul to sift each acre of dirt on both sides of the river. Good and decent souls as well as the rotten. Do you know anything about a place called Cave-in Rock?"

"Sure do," Fogg answered. "It's on the Ohio, upstream a ways from Cairo. Why?"

"A young trooper from Kentucky, now stationed at Fort Laramie, told me bad men used Cave-in Rock for a hideout."

"That's so," Fogg verified, nodding. "Big and Little Harpe—some say they were brothers, others think not—joined pirates operating out of the cave during

1798. But that didn't last long. They were too mean for the pirates. The pirates ran them off. Murdering butchers, they were. Anyhow, a posse of rangers caught up with the pair. Ranger justice was swift and final; Micajah 'Big' Harpe lost his head, but Wiley 'Little' Harpe escaped.

"Then Captain Samuel Mason came on the scene. Sam was slick and a sweet-talking southern gentleman from Virginia. He fought on the Pennsylvania frontier during the Revolution. Sam, his sons, daughters, their husbands and wives, all became holy terrors to people anywhere along the Mississippi from Cairo to New Orleans. Wiley cut off Sam's head in 1804. That wasn't the end to pirates, though. They're still around, only not organized as before. Do you think a pirate had something to do with the disappearances?"

"Something like that. It's been my experience that crooks lie awake nights thinking up new ways to turn a dollar. There might be a market for young, beautiful females. I know plenty of miners who would gladly pay every ounce of gold they have to get one."

"All this talk about stealing women is making me nervous," Elvira said. "If you gentlemen will excuse me, I'll take my leave."

The men rose. Fargo helped Elvira out of her chair. He said, "I'll be along shortly." She nodded. They watched her head for Vermont.

The waiter cleared the table of all food and drink except the wine. Bennett and Jance fired up cheroots, Fogg a curved stem calabash. Bennett produced a deck of playing cards. The men gathered at Fogg's end of the table. Farnsworth said he didn't want to play, but enjoyed watching a game of poker. Fogg suggested five-card stud. Jance shuffled, Fargo cut, the cards were dealt. Fogg opened with a red ace showing.

Bennett slid a sawbuck out to the middle of the table. He had the other red ace up. He didn't peek at his hole card. Without looking up, he asked Fargo,

"Miss Blassingame is your assistant? What does the lovely young woman do in that capacity, Mr. Fargo?"

Fargo looked at his hole card. It matched the deuce showing. He covered Fogg's opening bet. Without looking up from his cards, he answered, "Elvira is my bait."

7

The poker game broke up shortly before midnight.

Captain Fogg was the first to leave. "Dawn comes early for me, gentlemen." He knocked the ashes from the huge bowl of his pipe. "And I must take a turn around the decks before retiring up in Texas. Please, continue the game." He pushed back, picked up his money, then strode for the door leading to the gallery.

Two hands later, Philip Farnsworth said he felt sleepy and excused himself. George Jance played one more hand and lost to Fargo's two small pairs. Pushing back from the table, George said, "That's enough for me. I'll see you gentlemen at breakfast." He tucked what cash he had out into his inside coat pocket and left.

Fargo suggested he and Bennett move to the bar. The instant they moved away from the table, the waiter removed the wineglasses and tablecloth, spread a clean one, and started setting the table for breakfast.

Bennett ordered a whiskey, Fargo a shot of bourbon. Fargo said, "Captain Fogg mentioned 'up in Texas.' "

"Yes, that's what they call the officer's living quarters. Texas is on the hurricane deck above this one. As the story goes, a captain named the cabins after the states. He had one state too many. Texas was the most recent to join the Union. So he named the officer's quarters Texas. The name stuck and other captains started using it. The pilothouse is on top of Texas." He paused. "Bait?"

Fargo turned and rested the small of his back on

the edge of the bar. He looked down the full length of the saloon. Waiters were busy making things ready for the breakfast crowd. Finally, Fargo answered, "Elvira doesn't know my intentions yet. What's at the other end of the saloon?"

Bennett turned and followed Fargo's gaze. "The ladies' cabin. A place for them to lounge while gossiping out of hearing of us men."

"You have obviously traveled the Mississippi before."

Bennett chuckled. "More times than I care to remember."

"Captain Fogg implied you are a spy. Care to elaborate, deny or agree?"

"War between the North and South is coming, Mr. Fargo. It's a tinder box. One spark is all it will take for the fragile condition to explode. Nobody, least of all me, wants to see it happen, but hotheads are with us always. Yes, I am a spy . . . of sorts. While your mission is to find several women, mine is to find the tinder box and diffuse it. I'll start in New Orleans, then work my way to the East Coast. Others like me are working their way south from Washington. To be sure, our counterparts below the Mason-Dixon line are watching our troop movements. A clash is inevitable. All the ingredients are present to cause it to happen. Now for your problem. All of the young belles disappeared in Memphis. Have you ever been there?"

"No."

"Before conducting an exhaustive search east of the river, I would focus on the west. My opinion, of course, but you possess the nose, eyes, and ears of a cunning wolf. Like the wolf, you are better suited to hunt in timber, where the houses are few and far between. You can cover a great expanse of raw territory in record time. If you do not find them, then precious little time is wasted."

"I will give the advice serious consideration, if and when my bait doesn't get a nibble."

"You would let them take her?"

"I said nibble, not take. I'll keep Elvira under close

observation. I should say our stateroom." Fargo felt no need to expose his complete plan to a man he had met for the first time only a few hours ago. Bennett was the questioning type. For all Fargo knew the spy could be the culprit. The Trailsman obliquely changed the subject. "Where will the *Gypsy Queen* next stop? Cairo?"

Bennett laughed. Shoving his glass across the bar for Rafer to refill, he said, "The *Gypsy Queen*, like all other steamboats, will stop several times before arriving at Cairo." He sipped from the refill, then continued the explanation. "Fares and wood, Mr. Fargo, fares and wood. Captain Fogg is in direct competition with the other captains. Like them, he will pull ashore to pick up anyone who signals for passage. Then there is the fuel, wood for the boilers. Boilers burn wood at a rapid rate. Fogg will stop many times between here and New Orleans and send his mud clerk and a crew of roustabouts ashore to gather wood."

"That's interesting," Fargo mused. "Other than intermediary stops for wood and passengers, at which towns will he dock?"

"Between here and Memphis?"

Fargo nodded.

"Three. First, Cairo, then New Madrid, then Osceola."

"I've never heard of the last two."

"New Madrid is located in the notch in southern Missouri, just above Arkansas. Osceola is in Arkansas, on the west bank between New Madrid and Memphis. If I were you, I would start watching the cabin at Osceola."

The Trailsman had every intention of doing just that. "Well, Mr. Bennett, I think I will look in on my horse, then get some shut-eye. See you at breakfast."

"I'll be standing right here," Bennett said through an easy grin.

Fargo drank his shot glass of bourbon, slid fifty cents to Rafer, then left. Outside, he went to the hurricane deck and peered over the railing. If anyone on the main deck scaled the outer surface of the boat to get on the boiler deck, he would see them. Satisfied, he went higher, to the pilothouse.

Nobody was inside the lofty glass enclosure. He didn't enter, but looked in through the windows. Several cords with brass knobs on the ends hung from the ceiling. A huge spoked helm stood buried halfway in a wide slot at the front of the spacious enclosure. The half Fargo could see was as tall as a man. He looked down over the Vermont side of the boat. He knew this was the place to stand guard over his bait.

He left the pilothouse and went to the main deck. Roustabouts by the dozen labored under the watchful eye of a young man, who kept track of the cargo they brought aboard. As Fargo watched, the fellow made another entry in the ledger book he held.

At least a hundred poor folk huddled wherever they could find space among the swelling cargo on the main deck. Here a group of rowdy men shared a bottle of whiskey while rolling dice; there a man and wife and three small children clustered as one between two stacks of bags. The woman hummed a lullaby to soothe the youngsters to sleep.

Fargo threaded his way to the stern. Bales of hay and crates piled high stood on the starboard side of the steamboat. He climbed atop the bales and looked up. He saw a person could, with little effort, climb onto the boiler deck.

"What'cha looking for, mister?" Homer's voice asked.

Fargo dropped to the deck. Dusting his hands, he said lamely, "Looking across the river."

"You gonna see plenty more of it, sir, before this here boat gets to New Orleans."

Fargo gestured they go to the stalls. "Homer, have you been a stable boy on the *Gypsy Queen* very long? Say, er, the last six months or so?"

"Yes sir. My uncle Socrates, he's a waiter, he got me the job last December."

Fargo saw the Ovaro and appaloosa had been groomed. Rubbing his stallion's powerful rump, he said, "You see main-deck passengers come and go. Any of them make frequent trips between here and Memphis?"

"Not so I'd notice, sir. Maybe they do and maybe they don't. You'd have to ask the mud clerk. He ought to know."

"Mud clerk?"

"Yes sir. He's right over there." Homer pointed forward. 'He keeps count of what all comes aboard and leaves."

"I'll check with him." Fargo handed him a quarter. "You did a good job cleaning the horses. They shine like new coins." Fargo had seen what he wanted. He shot Homer a wink, then went to the gallery.

At the gallery door he looked in and saw William Bennett and the two bartenders conversing. Wanting to avoid Bennett, he moved down the railing to the outer door to Vermont, which he quietly opened. Elvira lay naked on the lower bunk. She stirred, rolled onto her side, and awakened.

Fargo sat in the chair to pull off his boots. "When did I become your assistant?" she murmured sleepily. "Does the job include enjoying sex with you? If so, I accept."

"If you can figure out how to get it done in that little bitty bed."

Encouraged, Elvira propped on an elbow and said, "Oh, you can bet where there's a will there is a way."

While he finished undressing, Fargo told her he wanted to use her as bait to catch the big, slippery fish. "At no time will your life be in danger," he assured her. "However, it will be necessary for him to enter the cabin before I arrive. My guess is he will gag you the first thing to prevent you from calling for help. Think you can put up with that long enough for me to burst in and catch him redhanded?"

"Fargo, I lived through a Cheyenne war chief's manhandling me. I'm sure I can put up with a mere gag. But I thought you wanted him to lead you to Regina McRae and the others?"

"The threat of dancing on the end of a rope will be enough to make him tell where to find them."

"And if he doesn't?"

"Then I'll let him go. I'll follow him wherever he goes."

"What makes you think he will settle on me?"

"Because each day you will strike sensual poses at the appaloosa's stall."

"Fargo, you're mean. But I'll do it. You know I will. Get over here and give me some lovin'."

They tried the bunk but found it impossible. Fargo was simply too large. He pulled her onto the hard floor.

The *Gypsy Queen's* throaty steam whistle jarred Fargo awake. Dawn's early gray filtered through the window shutters. Elvira, all but invisible in the heavy shadows, lay doubled up under the covers of the lower bunk, sound asleep. The whistle's long blast failed to rouse her. Fargo got off the floor and washed his hands and face. He dressed unhurriedly, ran his fingers through his hair, then slipped out onto the boiler deck.

Early risers lined the railing to watch the steamboat pull away from the wharf. Fargo went to the port side and joined others to watch. Resting his forearms on the railing, he looked down.

A ship's officer barked orders to roustabouts. They raised the landing platform and swung it aboard. Seconds later the long platform was stowed, sticking over the bow.

The steam engine throbbed. The officer shouted, "Take in all lines!"

Men on the dock slipped free the mooring lines tied to large cleats. Roustabouts quickly pulled the ropes aboard and coiled them on the main deck. Three short blasts on the whistle signaled the *Gypsy Queen's* departure. Her massive stern paddle wheel engaged.

The monkey rudders angled out toward the river. The *Gypsy Queen* slowly left the wharf. Moments later they were in midstream, the paddle wheel churning a white, frothy wake.

A waiter appeared on deck. As he walked around the deck, he chimed a small xylophone and repeated, "Breakfast is served, ladies and gentlemen."

Fargo watched the river traffic awhile longer, then drifted to the starboard side and returned to the Vermont. Elvira hadn't moved. He shook her. "Wake up, girl. You're missing breakfast."

"I don't want any," she mumbled. "I need sleep."

He yanked the covers back, whacked her fanny. "Get up, woman."

She slapped his hand. "Fargo, you're mean. Please, let me go back to sleep."

"See you at the breakfast table."

Captain Fogg entered from the gallery as Fargo pulled back the same chair he sat in at dinner the night before. Bennett was slumped over the bar, mumbling incoherently to himself.

Taking his seat at the head of the table, Fogg said wryly, "Poor old Bennett. I don't how he does it. I'll have to sober him up when we get to New Orleans. Again."

Socrates filled their coffee cups. Fargo watched the captain pour some into the saucer, then blow on it to cool the steaming brew a tad. As Fogg sipped from the saucer, Fargo asked, "Does Bennett make it a habit to get in his cups often? Is he really a spy?"

"No, he isn't a spy. At least I don't think he is. I accuse him of being one. I don't know what line of business Bennett is in. I do know he is wealthy. And, yes, Bennett always gets drunk first night aboard and stays that way until arriving in New Orleans."

"Does he catch the *Gypsy Queen* on a return trip?"

"No, never. I don't know where he goes, but the man always reappears in St. Louis, about a month later, sober as a judge."

Fargo changed the subject when he saw the Farnsworths coming. "Are there any young, attractive, single females on board?"

"Other than Miss Blassingame, no."

Fargo and Fogg stood while Farnsworth seated his wife. Socrates filled their coffee cups, then stepped back. Bellah immediately filled her plate with scrambled eggs, ham, and grits. Fogg brought the couple current on the topic of conversation. "Mr. Fargo asked if there were any unattached belles on board. I told him no." Glancing at Fargo, Fogg added, "I presume you mean first-class passengers."

"Yes. And please let me know if any board downstream."

The Jances arrived. Again the men rose. Jance seated his spouse. Glancing at Bennett, he commented, "What's wrong with William? Is he ill?"

Fogg chuckled. "No, he's passed out." Fogg motioned Jeansonne to approach. Fargo's wild-creature hearing eavesdropped Fogg's whisper in the black man's ear. "You and Rafer take Mr. Bennett to his cabin and tuck him into bed. Gently, now. Do you hear me, Jeansonne?"

The black man nodded.

Fargo was filled with a desire to be alone, to try to begin to make sense of what he'd seen so far aboard the *Gypsy Queen*. Glancing at the gallery door, he made his apologies. "Excuse me, folks. When my lady comes, please tell her I am on the main deck." He pushed back from the table and left.

He wandered to the gallery, where he sat to think and watch the ever-changing scenery glide by.

Mostly, he wondered about William Bennett, whether or not the man was what he claimed, where and how he got all the money Fogg said he had. Bennett obviously traveled a circuitous route . . . ending where? St. Louis? The nation's capital? New Orleans? How did he get to the other places he went? There were three other horses on the main deck. Was one of them Bennett's? Fargo made a mental note to ask Homer.

Was Bennett involved in some way with the kidnapper? Was the kidnapper already on board? Those last two questions opened up a completely new line of thought. Fargo would have to keep an eye on William Bennett, see if he ever went to the main deck, and if he did, then who he spoke with.

The *Gypsy Queen* entered a narrow stretch of the river, where gargantuan oaks formed a canopy. Fargo quit thinking about Bennett. The green tunnel captured his attention. For a brief moment, Fargo felt at home. A black couple and three youngsters fished from the west bank. Two older boys were launching a crudely made raft. They waved their straw hats at Fargo. He stepped to the side railing and waved back to them.

Elvira spoke from close behind him. "It's so beautiful here. I remember this part of the river from when we went to St. Louis. So restful. So peaceful."

"I agree."

She moved around him and stood, resting the small of her back against the railing. He saw she held a cup of coffee. She noticed him glance at it. "Captain Fogg and the others are worried they said something that offended you, Fargo."

"Did you have breakfast?"

"Oh, yes. Socrates filled my plate. I ate all the grits first."

They fell silent until the flash packet cleared the overhanging oak branches. The river widened immediately. A bend loomed ahead. The pilot hugged the east bank, so close that Fargo believed he could easily jump onto it. And that belief spawned another thought. Were there other close brushes with banks near Memphis? He'd soon find out. "Elvira, sit and wait for me. I'm going up to the pilothouse. Be back in a few minutes."

He took the stairs going up three at a time. He entered the pilothouse just when the pilot laid the helm over and came right, away from the bank. The *Gypsy Queen* responded to her four monkey rudders.

Two seamen, one on the port bow, nearest the bank, the other on the starboard side, swung weighted sounding lines out in front of the steamboat. The weights fast found the bottom of the river. Different colored rag strips told the line handlers the depth of the water on their respective sides of the *Gypsy Queen*. "Mark four!" shouted the one nearest the bank. "Mark four and a half!" shouted the other. The *Gypsy Queen* eased around the bend. The pilot visibly relaxed as he moved the giant wheel left and steadied up in midstream.

Only then did Fargo speak. "Close call?"

The pilot glanced over his shoulder at Fargo. "Not at all. There is a big sandbar just below the surface, jutting out from the west bank of this bend. Riffles on the water showed me where it is. What can I do for you? Mr. Fargo, isn't it?"

"Yes. How did you know?" Fargo stepped forward and looked over the pilot's shoulder.

"Captain Fogg told us we might see a big man dressed like a cowboy."

"I'm no cowboy, pilot."

"Name's Cy Hogan. The other pilot is Benjamin Kunkle. You'll pardon me for not looking at you. Gotta keep my eyes on the river to watch for danger signs up ahead: submerged logs, wrecked steamboats setting on the bottom, sandbars, and the like."

"Wrecked steamboats?"

"That's right. Boilers are bad about blowing up. When that happens, the whole shebang catches fire and runs aground, or sinks."

"Damnation, Cy, are you telling me—"

"It's a risky business, my friend. A pilot has to stay alert. Lives are at stake."

"Treacherous, huh?"

"You bet it is. A huge tree trunk only inches below the surface can rip a hull apart in the blink of an eye. Sandbars that weren't there on the last trip can be on the next."

"Far be it for me to draw your attention off the

river. I came to ask if you had to move in close to banks, say, during the night before docking in Memphis."

"You think that's when and where all those females disappeared?"

"I know that's when."

"I have to hug several banks, east and west, between Osceola and Memphis."

"Close enough for a stout man to pitch a woman onto the bank without hurting her?"

"Mr. Fargo, so close, in fact, that it scares me. The prevailing wind and current can cause this vessel, any vessel, to scrape the bank. When that happens, even a weakling could put a female ashore, then step onto the bank."

"You've answered my question. I believe that's how he does it."

"Got a suspect in mind?"

Hogan didn't need to know that William Bennett was a prime suspect. Fargo muttered, "No, not yet. Thanks for the river lesson, Cy."

"Anytime. Catch me when I'm off duty."

Fargo left the pilothouse and returned to the gallery. The breakfast crowd had moved outside to sit or stand in the shade and be cooled by a morning breeze. They were a quiet bunch, not anything like the crowd on the main deck. Fargo found Elvira sitting at a table in the sunlight at the front railing. Settling down into the chair across from her, he said, "I think I've seen how he does it."

"Oh? And?" She squinted one eye, the one to the sun.

"First, I gave thought to something you said last night after I awakened you."

"Before or after we made love? I'm not responsible for anything I say while in a state of euphoria."

"Before. You asked what if he doesn't tell me where he took those other young ladies. I've changed my mind, Elvira. I want him to lead me to the women, not tell me."

"Fargo, I don't like that idea. Using me as a bait to catch him, yes; letting him actually take me, no." She shook her head. After a long moment Elvira asked, "Where do you think they are?"

Fargo gazed thoughtfully downstream. "That many women suggests a lot of isolated men, men without women, men who do not want to be seen."

"Outlaws?"

"Or soldiers."

"Soldiers?"

"Maybe. A special group. Elite. Hidden in a secret place."

"Fargo, you amaze me. Really, you do. I would have never thought of soldiers." She touched his hand.

"On the other hand, what's to say the women stealer will strike this trip? He may be on another steamboat altogether."

Those sobering thoughts brought a lengthy silence. Finally, Elvira said, "I've been stolen twice." Rising, she added, "I suppose allowing it to happen a third time won't—"

"No," he blurted. "Twice is two times too many. If he's on board, I won't let him take you. I'll do it the hard way."

"Suit yourself. I think I'll go see what the ladies' cabin is like." Elvira kissed his cheek.

Fargo watched her walk inside the saloon. He marveled at her rump, knowing that if the sensual walk aroused him, then it would excite other men. He flagged down a waiter and ordered a cup of coffee. The Trailsman had much to think about. The gallery was as good a place as any to do it.

Before sunset, the *Gypsy Queen* pulled ashore four times—once for the mud clerk and his crew to gather firewood, the other three to pick up passengers. All four times Fargo watched with keen interest from the main deck. The pilot put the packet's bow to the bank and held it there. Roustabouts swung the long landing platform forward and lowered it to the ground. Twice, finely dressed family men came aboard after bidding their wives and children good-bye.

The third stop brought a family of four on board. Fargo listened to the husband negotiate the fare to Osceola with the chief clerk. The man didn't have the money. When he turned and herded his brood down the gangplank, Fargo halted them, saying, "Wait a minute." He paid the fares and palmed the husband a ten-dollar bill when the grateful man shook his hand.

"We got word Martha's mama is bad sick, maybe dying," the man explained. "They have a farm near Osceola. Least me and Martha can do is help get them through a rough time. Our kids are good field hands. We'll work our fingers to the bone to repay you, mister."

"Not necessary," Fargo replied. "I won more than that in a poker game last night."

"No, I want to make things right," the proud man insisted. "You were kind and generous to us. I'm indebted to you. I don't know when or how I'll get the money to you, but I will, somehow. What's your name? Mine's Seth Morgan."

"Skye Fargo. You can repay me by picking up fares for other poor souls in dire need."

Seth nodded. He shook Fargo's hand again, then led his wife and children aft.

At the same time Fargo felt good and saddened. He went to the gallery where he and Elvira sat to watch a peach-colored sunset. A waiter chiming dinner call broke Fargo's fixation on the sky and his thoughts. He lamented in a hollow tone, "I feel helpless. This waiting for something I know will happen is maddening. I've never felt so confined in all my life. Steamboats are not for me. I belong on the frontier and beyond."

"After dinner," Elvira began, "I'll relax you in our cabin."

True to her word, Elvira "relaxed" Fargo many times during the night. He awakened in midmorning, feeling no tension at all. Elvira had left the stateroom. Fargo washed up, dressed, and went on deck. The *Gypsy Queen* rode fast and easy on a straight stretch of the calm river. He found Elvira sitting in the shade in the gallery, a cup of coffee on the table next to her. Easing down into the chair across from her, he gestured the ever-present waiter to bring him coffee.

Elvira smirked. "Sleep well, big man?"

He nodded. "If Fogg pulled ashore, I didn't know it."

"He did twice after sunrise. Once during breakfast, the other about half an hour ago."

"Didn't feel a thing. Who came aboard?"

"When he came back to the table, he told us a family of five. I was out here the second time. A man and woman, both young, came aboard. All of them are main-deck passengers."

"You never said what went on in the ladies' cabin."

"Gossip. Pure gossip. The ladies were curious about me and you. Mrs. Bloxom posed all the questions: when and where we met, why we are traveling together, nosey stuff like that."

"What did you tell them?"

"What it was like to be captured by Indians. Mrs. Bloxom gasped and fanned her face. She asked for the details, so I told them what happened. Mrs. Bloxom fainted. The other ladies started fanning her and begged me to continue. Actually, it was kind of funny. But I didn't say anything about me being your bait. I don't think any of them know anything about the disappearances."

Fargo waited for the servant to fill his cup and leave, then he said, "That's good. Those old biddies will spread the word. By now, I wouldn't be surprised if every person on board didn't know you are single and . . ."

When he hesitated, Elvira said, "Go ahead and say it, Fargo. The blond hussy screws Indians."

"I was about to say the beautiful blonde knows how to take care of a man. Anyhow, I would like for you to spend more time in the ladies' cabin. Women sense things, little nuances, that we men do not. At night, after dinner, you can tell me what they talked about."

"Fargo, do you really want to hear about their boring husbands, brat children, and darling grand-babies?"

"No. You know what I mean. Will you do it? For me?"

"Yeah, I'll suffer through it, somehow. Oh, God, how I wish this was done and over. I, too, am catching your cabin fever. I long for the wide open spaces. I'm not cut out for fancy living. I detest holier-than-thou women, especially those who carry fans. I'm more comfortable around men, especially the rugged types, like you, Fargo. You make me feel like a woman, not a piece of warm meat. I need constant loving."

He started to tell her she would make someone an excellent wife. But he didn't. Instead, he said, "Wear the tight-fitting yellow dress when you go shopping in Cairo."

"I'm going shopping? First I heard about it."

"I want you seen in town, without me at your side."

"You want me to advertise my sexy self? That it, Fargo?"

"The bait has to be seen for the fish to come."

"Sharks, you mean."

"I mean if you tempt him, he might come aboard the *Gypsy Queen* rather than wait to catch another steamboat. I'm simply playing all the odds, Elvira. If you don't want to shop in Cairo, you don't have to."

"I'll go shopping. You know I will do my part. I'll swing my ass so well that it will load this boat with every fish in the pond."

Fargo chuckled. He knew she would do just that. Now that it was settled, he moved on to other subjects.

They sat and chatted until time for lunch. After eating, they returned to the gallery until it was time for Elvira to change clothes. He went with her to Vermont, where he sat on the lower bunk and watched her primp, then dress. The changes in the *Gypsy Queen*'s sounds signaled her arrival at Cairo. Patting Elvira's nicely rounded rump, Fargo announced it was time to go to the main deck.

They walked through the outer door in time to see roustabouts swinging the landing platform to the wharf on the portside. Fargo handed her twenty dollars to spend, then told her to go, that he would watch from the gallery.

He took a seat next to the railing on the port side, where he had an unobstructed view of the gangway. Passengers streamed off the boat. Among them shashayed Elvira, parasol in hand. Jubilant youngsters—boys in straw hats, girls in pigtails and wearing bonnets—ran on board. Fargo watched some dock hands tote cargo aboard and others carry off bulky items. The chief clerk made the new passengers wait on the wharf until the incoming cargo was on board. By the clothes they wore, Fargo guessed all the newcomers were main-deck passengers.

William Bennett staggered down the landing platform. A dock hand gave him a steadying hand. Fargo wondered if they had spoken. Bennett pushed the man aside and lumbered across the wharf and disappeared into the crowd.

Fogg came down from the pilothouse. "What's this, Mr. Fargo?" he intoned. "You're not going into town?"

"How long will we be here?"

"An hour. Long enough to get your land legs back."

"Bennett went ashore."

"Drunk or sober, he goes to the telegraph office to report his whereabouts to Washington."

"Do you know that for a fact?"

"No," Fogg admitted. "Only that he visits the telegraph office. You will see him go to others on down the line."

"There are no first-class passengers waiting to board?"

Fogg chuckled. "First class waits to arrive at the last minute. Are you looking for someone in particular?"

"No, I just thought it odd."

"You're watching for the culprit, aren't you, Mr. Fargo?"

"Yes. He has to come aboard somewhere."

"He may already be on board. Ever think of that, Mr. Fargo?"

"I have considered it. I've considered a whole lot of other possibilities, too."

"And?"

"And reached no definite conclusions. So, I sit and watch and wait. Sooner or later the bastard will make a false move and give himself away. They always do."

"Do you want to explain that?"

"It's like kids playing hide-and-seek. Those hiding really want to be discovered. They unconsciously leave little signs for those who seek to follow. The hiders watch the seekers from their hiding place, to see how warm they are getting. The clever seeker always fools and surprises them at the last second. I am one of the better seekers, Captain. I read signs other seekers miss. It begins before the game is played. I'm watching for the early signs, Captain Fogg."

"Good luck. I'm needed on the main deck. See you at the dinner table."

Fargo nodded and resumed observing the comings and goings on the wharf. After about half an hour, the pilot gave a short blast on the steam whistle. Within five minutes the passengers who had left the boat began streaming back on board. Elvira wasn't among them. Shortly, Fargo saw why. Her rolling rump was bringing in the fish. She shashayed around the corner of the warehouse. A gaggle of bulge-eyed men followed close behind. Fargo broke a wide grin.

Then he saw the tall woman following the group of giddy men at a discreet distance. Fargo guessed the shapely female's height at six feet, and she carried a perfect weight for her size. She wore a light-brown gingham dress, carried a matching parasol, and below the floppy straw hat on her head flowed dark-brown tresses that dangled below her broad shoulders. The lovely woman was no older than twenty-five. And if the group of men had turned and looked, they would have seen the same swinging ass that two horse riders behind her saw.

Fargo shifted his gaze onto the riders. One, obviously a madam, rode side saddle. She was beefy, wore a bright-red dress with a black, fuzzy hem and collar that matched, and too much makeup. A huge, muscular black man rode beside her. He wore a long, split-tailed black coat, pin-striped trousers, and a black top hat.

Behind them came a gaunt man riding a lop-eared mule, trailing two others.

Fargo leaned over the railing and watched Elvira blow a kiss to her admirers. They whistled, applauded, and threw their hats into the air. None followed her aboard.

When the tall brunette stepped onto the landing platform, the men crossed their hearts and feigned heart attacks. Two even fell onto the wharf and started kicking, as though in their final moment before death. The brunette smiled as she glanced up at Fargo, but she didn't turn around to see the men's antics.

The madam and her bodyguard—Fargo had decided that was his role—dismounted. She handed him the reins to her horse, a dun mare, then pushed her way through the silly-acting men and came aboard. The bodyguard and horses followed.

Before dismounting from the mule, the gaunt fellow waited for the group of men to disperse. Fargo saw why. The man was crippled in the left leg. He used a crutch to help him walk. He was dressed for main-deck passage. Baggy, much-worn pants were tied with a frayed rope around his waist. A red, long-sleeve shirt, also oversized and filthy as sin, covered his upper body. On his head was a strange-looking black hat. The brim had been cut off with little regard to neatness. Only the felt crown had been saved, and it was misshapen.

Long, soot-black hair hung below his shoulders. Fargo imagined the cripple had never seen a razor. His straight beard flowed to his stomach. Dark, sunken eyes stared from beneath bushy black eyebrows. In a word, the gaunt-faced cripple looked pitiful.

Each of the two mules he trailed carried two deep and wide cane baskets. The lids covering them prevented Fargo from seeing what was inside.

The fellow hobbled aboard.

As the roustabouts were swinging the landing platform on deck, Bennett staggered into view.

8

At dinner that night, the tall brunette occupied the seat normally used by William Bennett. William didn't show up for dinner. Neither was he at the bar. Fogg explained Bennett was in his stateroom, and left it at that. The captain proceeded to introduce the brunette, whom he obviously knew, to the others at the table. "Miss Gloria LeBeaux's parents have a cotton plantation near Natchez," he said for openers. "Gloria, I'll start with the person sitting on your left, then go around the table." The three women sat on her left, the men across the table from them.

When Fogg introduced Fargo as the Trailsman, Gloria's doe-brown eyes widened. Fogg moved on to Philip, then George Jance.

During the course of the leisurely eaten meal, Bellah and Florence became Gloria's chief questioners. "I've been attending school in Boston," Gloria explained. "Miss Lucille Posey's Finishing School for Proper Ladies, to be exact. My parents thought it best for me to learn all about grace and charm. I was, still am, a tomboy." She glanced at Fargo. "What's a trailsman? You look like a cowboy."

Elvira answered, "He's not a cowboy."

Gloria's eyes cut to Elvira. "Oh? Then, what is he? Are you his . . . companion, Miss Blassingame?"

Fargo saw Elvira's uneasiness. He hurried to explain, "A trailsman breaks paths for others to follow. I rescued Elvira from Miniconju Sioux after she was captured by Cheyenne. I am escorting her to Mem-

phis. Like you, she is a tomboy. Fights like a man."
He looked at Elvira and shot her a wink.

Elvira smiled. She served notice on the brunette.
"You might as well know, since everyone else does.
Fargo and I share the same cabin."

Bellah blurted, "Tell Gloria about your ordeal with
the savage Cheyenne war chief—"

"No," Gloria interrupted. "I don't want to hear
about it. Please, leave it to my vivid, creative imagination." She threw a grin to the blonde, then looked at
Fargo.

He saw a burning passion in Gloria's eyes. So did
Elvira, who said matter-of-factly, "There really isn't
much to tell. What did you do in Boston . . . other
than attend finishing school?"

The not-so-charming brunette answered matter-of-
factly too, "Like you, I spent most of my time flat on
my back."

Bellah and Florence chorused a gasp. But the
madam, sitting immediately behind Elvira, smiled
when she turned to look at the two verbal duelers.

Things were getting out of hand. Fargo changed the
subject. "When do we arrive at Memphis, Captain
Fogg?"

"That depends on how many stops I have to make
for firewood and passengers. Normally it takes three
days from Cairo."

"I saw a crippled man come aboard at Cairo."

"We call him Crutch. His real name is Barlow.
Amos Barlow is a regular. He makes moonshine. Best
I ever had. Real smooth. Crutch boards in Memphis.
You saw the cane baskets?" When Fargo nodded,
Fogg explained, "They're filled with jugs of moonshine. Crutch has steady customers between Memphis
and Cairo, where he gets off the *Gypsy Queen*. Then
he takes a steamboat up the Ohio. I don't know how
far he goes, but he rarely misses this boat when it
returns from Minneapolis."

"I thought you said you didn't have any regular
passengers," Fargo quizzed.

"I meant not any you would be interested in." He nodded toward the hefty madam. "Like her."

The madam twisted around and said, "You talking about me again, you old coot? If you are, speak up so I can hear and set the record straight."

"Madame Broussard," Fogg began, "why don't you join us? Yes, I'm talking about you."

She got up and wedged her chair between Elvira's and Bellah's. Madame Broussard scanned the men's faces, then said, "I own a brothel in Nashville. My girls are the best in the business." She locked onto Fargo's lake-blue eyes. "I saw you eyeballing me and Buford on the dock. The answer is no, Jack isn't my lover."

"Well, of all the nerve," gasped Florence.

"Hush," Philip quickly replied. He looked at Broussard. "Madam, we will appreciate it if you would control your language."

Broussard laughed. "Fogg, this table is too uppity for me." She got up and put her chair back in its original position at the other table.

Gloria said, "I like her. She isn't phony."

Fargo wasn't so sure. He said, "If you ladies will excuse me, I must look in on my horse."

"You have a horse?" Gloria queried.

For the moment, Fargo ignored her question. Moreover, he knew it was an attempt to keep him at the table. Gloria LeBeaux had been glancing naughtily at him. While the tall plantation owner's daughter was definitely desirable, and obviously available, Fargo had other pressing matters to tend to. The eager brunette would have to wait.

He said, "Elvira, why don't you entertain these good people while I'm gone? Play something on that big piano." Pushing back from the table, he looked at Gloria. "To leap-frog your question and answer all the others it would trigger, I'm looking for somebody. A horse is needed where I'm going. Captain Fogg will fill you in." He rose, nodded, and left.

Fargo went to the main deck. Jack Buford stood at

the port bow railing, watching the east-bank scenery slip by. Fargo joined him. When Jack started to walk away, Fargo said, "Jack Buford, I want to talk to you. Can you spare me a few minutes?"

Jack's belly laugh was more of a throaty rumble than anything else. In a deep bass voice he answered, "Mister, I ain't going nowhere. We can talk all night if you want."

Fargo liked him immediately. "I gather you and Madame Broussard make this trip often. Is that correct?"

"Yes, sir, it is. What do you want to know 'bout Miss Honey? I've been with her a long time."

Damn, Fargo thought, this man is perceptive as hell. He gets right to the point. "Honey mentioned having a brothel in Nashville."

"She has two. One in Nashville, the other near Cave-in Rock. She visits the one at Cave-in every month. Cynthia Nagle runs it for Honey. By the way, what's your name, if you don't mind telling me?"

"Skye Fargo." He extended his hand.

Gripping Fargo's hand, Jack asked, "Why you interested in Miss Honey?"

Buford's firm handshake put Fargo even more at ease. He decided Jack Buford could be trusted with sensitive information. Besides, time was running out. Fargo had to know certain things, missing pieces to the puzzle, things that Jack might know. "I'm not interested in Honey, or her brothels. I *am* interested in William Bennett. Do you know him?"

"We've met. Miss Honey, being in first class and all, she knows him better than I do. What do you want to know 'bout Mr. Bennett?"

"His line of work."

Jack shook his head. "I don't know 'bout that. You'd have to ask her. All I know is Mr. Bennett comes from somewhere back East. Boston, I think. Someplace like that. He catches the boat in St. Louis and goes to New Orleans. Right regular, he does."

"Do you not think it odd that he would meet the

Gypsy Queen in St. Louis? Seems to me it would make more sense for him to take a steamboat operating on the Ohio and meet her at Cairo."

"Now that you mention it, I agree. Taking the Ohio to Cairo would be faster. Maybe he has a route that puts him in St. Louis."

"I'll ask Miss Honey. Do you know women have been disappearing off the *Gypsy Queen* and the *Dulce Girl*?"

Buford stiffened. "If you think Miss Honey and me took them, you're wrong."

"Relax, Jack. I'm not accusing either of you. I suspect Bennett. My problem is figuring out how he does it. He has to have confederates."

"I know they always turn up missing at Memphis. You a lawman?" Buford asked.

"No. A man gave me the job of finding his young daughter. She was on this packet."

"You think all them young beauties are together?"

Fargo nodded. "The question is, on which side of the river? Bennett suggested I search west."

"I don't know. They could be anywhere. I'll keep my eyes open for you. Confederates, huh? Never thought 'bout it that way. But it makes sense. If Mr. Bennett is involved."

"Jack, it has been good chatting with you. Keep what we discussed under your hat." Fargo shook Buford's hand again, then went aft to the horse stalls.

Homer greeted him. He sat on top of one side of the stalls and watched Fargo walk around the Ovaro, rubbing the stallion's face, scratching his rump and withers. "Fine horse, mister. Gentle as can be. Nothing like Crutch's mules. They're mean as hell."

Fargo looked at the three mules stalled adjacent to the Ovaro. Honey's dun and Jack's gray dappled gelding occupied the two stalls next to the mules. He noticed the baskets of moonshine stood against crates on the starboard side of the *Gypsy Queen*. He stepped to them, lifted a lid, and looked inside. The basket was filled with gallon jugs.

Crutch appeared next to Fargo. Crutch raised another lid. In a low, raspy tone of voice he drawled, "I get a dollar a jug, stranger." He brought out a jug and handed it to Fargo. "Pull the cork and take a swig. Got four jugs left. One swig and you'll buy one."

Fargo took a swig. Fogg was right. The moonshine was smooth. Excellent, in fact. "You sold me," Fargo said through an easy grin.

"I knowed I would." Crutch shot him a crooked grin.

"Captain Fogg mentioned you had a route."

"Yes, sir. A long one."

"Up the Ohio?"

"Yes, sir. I go as far as Cave-in Rock."

"Then you know Madame Broussard?"

"I know her. Sinful woman, she is. She paints her face. All of 'em do."

Fargo nodded. He started to walk away.

"That'll be one dollar, sir," Crutch reminded Fargo as he looked at the jug in his hand.

"My apologies." Fargo fumbled two fifty-cent pieces out of his pocket. Handing the coins to Crutch, he asked, "Where's home?"

"Near the Loosahatchie River, 'bout twenty miles uther side of Memphis. Good night, sir." Crutch pocketed the money.

Jug in hand, Fargo moved back to the stalls. He asked Homer, "You know Jack Buford?"

"I tend his horses."

"But do you know him?"

"A little bit."

"Crutch?"

"Naw, sir. Nobody *knows* Crutch."

"Where's Buford from?"

"Till Miss Honey got him, Jack was a slave on Mulberry Plantation."

"Where's that?"

"Memphis. Out a ways. By the Loosahatchie."

Homer, Fargo concluded, knew much, more than

the youngster himself realized. Fargo tested the depth of the lad's knowledge. "Do you know anything about Mr. William Bennett? Where he goes? What he does?"

"A little bit. Mr. Bennett is a sheep dressed up like a wolf. He says I'm gonna be free. He says all the slaves are gonna be free."

"Did he tell you that? I mean, does he come down here and say those things?"

"Oh, no sir, I ain't never seen Mr. Bennett. He stays up on boiler deck. He's first class. Uncle Socrates, he told me."

So, Fargo thought, Bennett and Socrates get together. "Madame Broussard. Homer, do you know how she gets the girls who work for her?"

Homer tensed. He dropped off the side of the stall and shook his head. "I don't know anything 'bout that, sir."

Fargo saw Homer was uncomfortable. Homer did not want to discuss this line of thought any further. Fargo put him at ease, saying, "I have never traveled the Mississippi before. There are a lot of interesting people on this boat." He tossed the youngster a grin, patted his stallion's rump, then walked away.

Moving on, he left the main deck and returned to the saloon. Elvira sat at the piano, playing it for the crowd surrounding her. She looked happy. He stepped to the bar, where Bennett slouched, a glass of whiskey in front of him. Rafer shook his head dolefully. Fargo ordered a shot of bourbon and set the gallon of moonshine on the bar.

"I see you visited Crutch," Rafer began. "That white lightning of his is mighty potent stuff." Rafer chuckled, then continued, "His mules drink it. Crutch gives 'em a nip now and then to settle 'em down."

Bennett slurred, "Have we arrived in Memphis?"

"No," Fargo answered.

Bennett straightened up and looked toward the piano. Fargo watched him rub his face, then blink several times, obviously trying to focus. Finally, Bennett mumbled, "Damn, that woman is tall. Who is she?"

Fargo glanced at the brunette standing, looking over Elvira's shoulder. "If you mean the brunette, her name is Gloria LeBeaux."

"Is she married?"

"No."

Bennett asked Rafer for a refill, then took the glass and drifted up behind Gloria. Apparently he said something to her. When she turned to face him, both smiled. Fargo watched them talk briefly, then leave through the gallery door. Bennett shot Fargo a wink that implied a successful conquest.

After watching and listening to Elvira play for the crowd for a while, Fargo went to the gallery for a breath of fresh air before retiring for the night. Bennett and Gloria weren't there. Fargo looked down the port railing first. Neither were they there. He checked the starboard side. Gloria was unlocking an exterior door about midway between the gallery and stern. Bennett rested his back to the railing. Gloria disappeared inside the cabin. Bennett lurched to follow her.

Fargo returned to the saloon. Elvira was having a whale of a good time, leading the gathering in song as her nimble fingers raced over the keyboard. He didn't interrupt the gaiety. After having another shot of bourbon, he took his moonshine to the Vermont and crawled into the upper bunk.

During early dawn the *Gypsy Queen* docked at New Madrid. Fargo dressed quietly so as not to awaken the pianist, then went out on deck. A few people stood at the dock end of the landing platform. Roustabouts hurried to carry off cargo and bring more on board. He watched who came aboard and who got off. The platform was raised and swung on deck. Three toots on the whistle, and the pilot pulled away. Fargo went to the saloon.

He immediately sensed something was wrong, as it should not be. Waiters were busy bringing silver trays laden with breakfast from the galley into the saloon.

That wasn't it, he told himself. He sat at the captain's table, touched his cup, and glanced about for Socrates. The waiter was nowhere in sight. Fargo fidgeted a few moments while waiting for Socrates to arrive. Restless, he got up and went to the gallery. His mind raced as he stood at the front railing. Trusting his instincts that something was out of place, he glanced to the stairs leading to the main deck. Main deck? he thought.

Going to the main deck, Fargo took the stairs three at a time, then walked casually, as though out for a morning stroll, so as not to be overly conspicuous while checking on things.

The Morgan family lay sleeping, nestled between two tall stacks of crates. An older man sat rubbing his face and eyes awake. Fargo peered between two piles of fifty-pound bags. Jack Buford and Bennett stood conversing at the starboard rail. The vessel's engine made it impossible for his wild-creature hearing to eavesdrop their conversation. He began working his way closer.

Coming around a stack of boxes, he saw Socrates standing with Homer next to the mule's stalls. When Fargo looked away, Crutch the moonshiner rose out of the heavy shadows next to the buffalo hides and looked directly at him. Neither spoke.

After a long pause, Fargo returned his gaze toward the stable boy and his uncle. Socrates was no longer there. Fargo moved parallel to the starboard side, toward the bow. He glimpsed Socrates hurrying up the stairs.

The chief clerk's voice spoke from behind Fargo. "Lost, Mr. Fargo?"

"Hardly, Mr. Post. Only taking my morning constitution before having breakfast. When do we arrive at Osceola?"

"If the river is good to us, around midnight, Mr. Fargo. Did you change your mind about getting off in Memphis?"

"No. Just curious."

"If you leave at Osceola, I'll return partial payment for passage."

"Not necessary, Mr. Post."

Post nodded. Fargo watched him join two roustabouts over by the landing platform. The big man's eyes scanned the people and cargo a final time before he returned to the saloon. Bennett and Buford still stood talking at the port railing. Neither noticed him.

Fogg, the Jances, and the Farnsworths sat at the breakfast table. Fargo joined them. Socrates filled Fargo's cup with steaming coffee. Fargo decided Socrates' earlier absence was what had left him with the uneasy feeling.

Shortly, Elvira came to the table. Right off, Fargo noticed something bothered her. She ate in silence, a faraway look in her eyes. Several times she paused with her fork of scrambled eggs and stared blankly, as though something terrible had happened and she was afraid to mention it. Fargo concluded that whatever it was, it regarded Gloria LeBeaux. He didn't probe.

Gloria didn't show up for breakfast, but did for lunch. She sat at a table two rows aft of the captain's. Out of the corner of his eye, Fargo noticed Gloria watching him.

At dinner, Elvira was as sullen as she was during breakfast and lunch. Fargo took her out onto the gallery. "Elvira, you're in a rotten mood. Want to talk about it?"

Sighing, she shrugged.

"Look at me, Elvira. Tell me what's bothering you? Is it Gloria LeBeaux? Do you think I'm seeing her?"

Elvira looked away, shook her head.

"Do you still want to go through with my plan?"

She nodded. After a long pause, she muttered, "It's just that after tonight it will be all over between you and me. Dammit, Fargo, I'm in love with you, and I know it cannot be . . ." She started crying.

Fargo realized she was feeling melancholy. He embraced her. She hugged him tightly and sobbed, trembling. "Oh, Fargo, it seems so long ago when you rescued me. So long ago. Now, suddenly, it's over. What will I do without you? Oh, what will I do?"

He didn't have a ready answer. This lengthy involvement with the shapely blonde was out of the ordinary for the Trailsman. But like tumbling dominoes, one thing had led to another and kept them together. She had professed her love for him, the kind of love that could only end at an altar. Fargo had no intention of doing that. He was born to roam. The wilderness was his home, the creatures in it were his relatives, the forests, mountains, streams, and valleys of wildflowers, his domain. All of this, and more, flashed rainbowlike in his brain.

He decided it was up to him to make a clean break. It would hurt her, yes, but he knew Elvira possessed an inner strength that would see her through that hurt.

He said, "Elvira, things have gotten out of hand between us. You have your life to lead, and I have mine. They go in two different directions. When we arrive in Memphis tomorrow, I'll see to it that you get transportation to Atlanta.

"And I have changed my mind about using you for bait. I'll do it the hard way. In the meantime, lock yourself inside Vermont. Tonight, I'm playing cards with the boys in the saloon."

She pulled back and gasped, "You mean we won't make love . . . ever again?"

"I don't feel up to it."

"You bastard," she spat, and slapped his face. "Go to her! See if I care." Elvira spun and strode into the saloon.

Rubbing his cheek, Fargo realized that Gloria Le-Beaux was Elvira's problem, after all. He tarried on the gallery awhile longer, studying the night sky, which was overcast. It looked like it might rain. A moisture-laden, brisk wind blew from ahead of the *Gypsy Queen*. Fargo moseyed into the saloon.

At the bar, he saw Bennett and four men engaged in a game of five-card draw.

Jeansonne asked, "The usual, Mr. Fargo?"

"No. Make it a shot of whiskey this time." Jeansonne poured as Fargo asked, "Does the pilot pull ashore during a hard rain?"

"Sometimes. Mostly, he gets in the middle and slows down and waits for it to lighten up."

Drink in hand, Fargo drifted to the cardplayers. Bennett said, "Open seat, Mr. Fargo. Want in?"

Fargo sat and put fifty dollars on the table. Two hours later his poke increased by sixty dollars, and it began raining. Shortly thereafter the stern paddles slowed, the whistle tooted. Nonplussed, Bennett explained, "We've coming into Osceola."

Fargo played one more hand, lost twenty to three queens, then left the game and went to the main deck to watch the docking. The wind had laid and the rain had changed to a steady drizzle. Roustabouts swung and lowered the landing platform to the wharf on the starboard side. The chief clerk motioned the six passengers waiting to board to proceed. They hurried to comply. All bought main-deck tickets. Roustabouts began off-loading cargo, then brought even more aboard on their return trips. Fargo watched the mud clerk's crew fetch firewood for the boiler.

Captain Fogg appeared next to Fargo. "Nasty night, ain't it, laddie?"

"Will we stay docked till the pilot can see his way?"

"No. He can see both banks. Do you think the woman-stealer is on board?"

"Might be. Might not. One thing is for damn sure: he's mighty clever. Anyone who can steal females right in front of you has my respect. Stealing so many is nothing short of magic, I'm keeping my eyes open, Captain. I will catch him if he is on board."

Fogg grunted, "Good luck, laddie," then stepped to the chief clerk.

Fargo moved to the starboard side, where he could have a clear view of it and the wharf. By the time the pilot had moved the flash packet into midstream, Fargo hadn't seen anything suspicious. He returned to the card game. After playing two hands, the hairs on the nape of his neck tingled. Why? he wondered. He glanced at the bar. Rafer and Jeansonne stood talking to Socrates. That wasn't what had raised them. He shifted his gaze to the Vermont. Folding with two pair, he left the game and went to look in on Elvira.

He found her curled up under the covers, sound asleep. He checked the outer door to make sure she had locked it. She had. Satisfied, he closed and locked the inner door behind him, then went out to the gallery, where he sat to watch and wait. The drizzle had cleared. The calm air hung muggy. Fargo's clothes clung to him like damp washrags. The hairs on his nape tingled again. Somebody was watching him. He was sure of it.

Slowly, he scanned the deserted gallery. Then he spotted the silhouette of half of a person's head. The person stood on the starboard side, peeking around the corner of the gallery at him. As Fargo strained to see who, the head pulled back. He said, "I know you're there. I'm looking straight at you."

The silhouette of a long, slender, bare leg hooked around the corner. Then a slender arm appeared. The index finger on the hand crooked and gestured him to come. Fargo reckoned the enticing finger belonged to Elvira. He stepped to the corner.

Gloria LeBeaux stood buck-naked. She purred, "Want some of me, big man? I'm hot and ready."

He became aroused instantly. "Honey, you sure know how to tempt a man. How could I refuse?"

Gloria pressed her body to his and kissed him, openmouthed, her hot tongue working vigorously inside his mouth. The tall brunette was a wildcat, all right. Fargo had a hundred and fifty pounds of naked flesh on his hands, and every ounce of it begged to see if he could satisfy the hellion's lust. He would damn sure try.

His free hand cupped her shapely ass and pulled, fusing her body to his.

Gloria shuddered, moaned, "Oh, goddamn, that does feel good."

"Why don't we go to your cabin?" he suggested.

She led him to her door. Nudging it open with a heel, she started undoing the buttons on his fly.

Fargo coaxed the eager woman inside. "Honey, don't rush me. I'll be here till morning."

He removed his hat and gun belt. She backed against the far wall. Fargo pulled off his shirt.

She cupped her heavy breasts.

Fargo pulled off his boots, then released his belt buckle.

Gloria's breathing quickened. She slid a hand to her bushy patch and fondled her crotch.

Fargo removed his Levi's and underwear. His throbbing prong popped free.

Gloria gasped, raised one knee to her belly, and invited Fargo to take her where she stood.

When Fargo came to her, she clamped the bent leg to his hard buttocks. The head of his rock-hard member found her hot slit. One shove was all it took for him to plunge into the juicy opening.

Gloria grunted, "Oh, goddamn, that hurts, but don't stop. Please, plow deeper . . . all the way. Owee, that's it! Yes, yes, that's it." She clung to him like creeping ivy, wiggled her hips to capture all of him.

Fargo grabbed her buttock cheeks and thrust to a new depth.

She moaned her ecstasy, "Oh . . . oh . . . faster, big man. Don't quit. Please don't. I'm on fire." She raised and curled the other leg around his buttocks.

Fargo nuzzled her breasts. She fed the left one into his mouth, murmured, "Suck hard, big man. Oh, that feels so good. Suck it hard. Oh, my God . . . Jesus . . . Jesus. Wonderful!"

Gloria was bucking now, twisting and squirming on the ironlike prod, pumping, shoving and bouncing— doing anything and everything to increase her joy. Her head lolled, she gasped constantly. Her fingers twisted in his hair, she bit his ears, shoulders, and neck; she clawed his back. Fargo's powerful, steady strokes rode high on her tunnel, stretched the already widened blood-swollen lower lips, glided rhythmically in and out, in and out of her fiery, wet sheath.

Through clenched teeth she moaned, "Now, big man! Now . . . now! Explode with me . . . I'm coming, I'm coming!" She gasped, "Oh . . . oh . . . oh!"

He felt her buttock muscles tense, her legs tighten viselike, her fingernails dig into his back, her mighty contractions seize around his member. Fargo's volcano erupted.

Gloria's body fell limp. Totally exhausted, the heavily perspiring hellcat clung to him. Her legs came down and he slipped out of the wet, velvetlike casing. They kissed.

Gloria stepped to the washbasin. Dampening the washcloth, she cooed, "You're good, big man. Best I ever had." She clamped a towel high between her silky, smooth thighs, brought the wet cloth to him, and cleaned him up. Afterward, she drank from a jug of moonshine on the table by the bed.

"Take it easy on that stuff," Fargo warned. "It's got a hell of a bite."

"I don't care. I want to glow, big man. Glow like a little lightning bug in the springtime. I feel warm all over." She brought the mouth of the jug to hers and swilled.

That's when Fargo saw a glow of a different kind filter through the shutters on the window, a diffused, eerie, foreboding glow.

Colt in hand, he opened the outer door. Fog as thick as pea soup greeted him. He stepped outside. The pulsating glow came from a fireball suspended in the fog up near the gallery and out a ways from the port railing. Fargo couldn't believe his eyes. He stretched for the railing, grabbed it, and saw the same eerie glow from another fireball on the starboard side. The *Gypsy Queen*'s big brass bell above the pilothouse tolled four times. The steamboat set dead in the water.

Fargo groped his way back inside the stateroom. Gloria sat on the lower bunk, drinking moonshine. She slurred, 'C'mere, big guy. I wanna fuck again.''

He reckoned that was all she had learned at the charm school. He dressed quickly. Gloria, jug in hand, had staggered to lean against the doorjamb and peer out into the fog. He told her. "You're too drunk to go out. You could easily fall overboard. In this fog, it would be impossible to save you." He pulled her to the bunk. Gloria passed out before he could cover her nakedness. Fargo closed and locked the outer door, then went into the saloon.

Bennett and two men were still playing cards. Other than them, the saloon stood deserted.

Fargo strode to the gallery door. Outside, he fumbled his way up to the pilothouse. The fog was thinner at this height. He now saw the two fireballs were encased in huge iron baskets. He opened the pilothouse door and stepped inside. Fogg stood looking over the pilot's shoulder. Fargo asked, "What's going to happen?"

Fogg turned and answered, "Well, laddie, Cy Hogan here is fixing to beach her. Isn't that right, Cy?"

"Yep," Cy answered, "Soon as I get my bearings. Never saw such a fog. One minute it wasn't there, next minute it was. Caught me with my pants down, it did."

"Where are we?" Fargo inquired.

Cy replied, "Reckon we'd be 'bout twenty miles downstream of Osceola. What do you figger, Cap'n?"

"More or less," Fogg guessed.

The pilot rang the bell four times, then pulled a funnel attached to a hollow tube to his mouth. He shouted into the funnel, "Ahead slow, Mr. Finch. I'm going ashore. Stop when you feel the bump."

Fargo left the pilothouse and went to the Vermont. After checking to see if Elvira was all right, he went to Gloria's stateroom and looked in on her. She lay facedown, her left arm hanging over the side of the bunk. Satisfied that all was well, Fargo moved to the gallery, where he waited for the *Gypsy Queen* to bump against the bank.

Soon, he heard roustabouts raise and extend the landing platform forward and beyond the bow. Fargo knew the bump would soon follow. He held a hand in front of his face. He couldn't see it. He started moving it closer and closer toward his eyes. He felt his breath on his palm before seeing a vague outline of his hand.

The paddles began whumping slowly. Although Fargo couldn't see it happening, he sensed the pilot had turned the flash packet toward the bank.

Suddenly there was a flurry of activity down on the main deck. Deckhands and roustabouts cursed the fog as they shuffled about. That brought a chorus of protests from the other passengers. The pilot clanged the bell, tooted the whistle. Two different voices, both in the bow—one on the portside, the other on the starboard—began chanting the depth of the water.

Fargo heard someone sneaking toward him. His gun hand automatically gripped the Colt's handle. A groping hand grazed his left arm. He drew the Colt and jammed its nuzzle into the person's gut.

Madame Broussard screamed and Fargo heard her collapse onto the gallery deck.

A fight broke out on the main deck.

People yelled protests.

Fargo pulled Broussard to her feet, fumbled for and found a chair to sit her into. As he patted her face to bring her around, the *Gypsy Queen* mushed into the bank.

The gallery door opened and closed.

Bennett said, "Anybody out here?"

Fargo answered, "Over here, William. Madame Broussard fainted. I'm trying to rouse her. Give me a hand. I need to go to the main deck."

"Main deck? What the hell for?"

Captain Fogg bellowed from the hurricane deck, "All right, Mr. Stinson, get your boots muddy."

Stinson's voice shouted from the main deck, "Okay, you men, Captain says go ashore and get firewood. Watch your footing on the gangplank."

Boots scraped as the mud clerk and his crew moved down the landing platform.

The gallery door opened again. This time it stayed open. In the light spilling from the saloon Fargo saw several hazy silhouettes emerge. Passengers had awakened and were curious to know what the racket was all about.

George Jance's voice spoke. "Hell, I can't see anything. I'm going back to bed."

Madame Broussard spat angrily, "Stop slapping my face, whoever you are."

Bennett chuckled.

Fargo groped his way down the stairs to the main deck. The fog hid everything. He couldn't imagine how the mud clerk's crew could find the landing platform, much less go ashore to find and gather firewood. The twin fireballs cast enough diffused light for him to make out the fuzzy silhouettes of cargo and people gathered in the bow. Fargo stepped onto the gangplank and peered into the fog.

A man hurrying ashore brushed against Fargo. Off-balance, the man slipped and came close to falling in the water. Fargo grabbed the man's arm and pulled him erect. Nose-to-nose he saw it was Jack Buford. "Where are you going, Jack?" he questioned suspiciously.

Buford became evasive. "Why, er, nowhere. Just looking. That's all. You can let go now. Thanks for helping me up."

"I don't think I would venture out in this soup. Might get lost."

"Maybe you're right."

Buford squirmed around him and quickly vanished in the fog on the main deck.

Fargo listened to the mud clerk's men curse the fog

for a while, then backed off the landing platform and into a pair of arms, which seized around him.

At first he thought he'd collided with Jack Buford, but it was Mr. Post who said, "Pardon me. Didn't see you coming." He released his hold on Fargo.

Fargo replied, "No apology necessary, Mr. Post. I'm blind as a bat, too. Are some of the passengers getting off here?"

"Not that I know of. I'm making sure nobody sneaks aboard in this shit."

"Then you are going to stand here till we leave?"

"You bet. Nobody is cheating this vessel out of a penny. Not if I have anything to say about it."

Comfortable that nobody carrying a naked blonde or brunette ashore could go unnoticed by Post, and the landing platform was the only way to get ashore, Fargo returned to the saloon. Just about everyone sat, drinking coffee poured by the sleepy-eyed waiters. Fargo hurried to the Vermont and peeked inside. Elvira hadn't moved. He gently closed her door and went to Gloria's. She, too, lay buried under the covers. Satisfied that all was as it should be, he moved to and sat at Socrates' table.

Socrates smiled as he poured the big man a cup of coffee, then he said, "Morning, Mr. Fargo, sir. Been out, looking at the fog?"

"Yes. Does this happen often?"

"No sir. Worst fog I ever seen. Anything else, sir? Want me to see if the biscuits are ready to come out of the oven?"

Fargo shook his head. Stirring his coffee, he watched Socrates join another waiter.

All night Fargo sat and drank coffee. After each cup he got up and looked in on Elvira and Gloria. Nothing was amiss. He decided the culprit wasn't on board. He dozed off to sleep.

The steam whistle awakened him. He rushed outside and saw the fog had lifted and the *Gypsy Queen* was backing away from the bank. He hurried to check on the blonde and brunette once more. Each lay on her side, facing the wall with her head under the covers.

After having a quick breakfast, Fargo stood at the forward gallery railing to watch the scenery. Fogg came down from the hurricane deck and joined him. "I guess he's not on board," Fargo mused.

"Doesn't appear so. Well, laddie, I haven't had my breakfast yet." The captain turned to leave.

Fargo stopped him. He'd seen something strange, mighty strange. He pointed toward several one-gallon jugs bobbing in a riffle on the starboard side, near the west bank.

Fogg grunted, "There's a sandbar inches below the surface."

As they watched, several more jugs washed into the riffle. A movement of a low-hanging oak branch caught Fargo's attention. Focusing on the branch, he saw a black youngster crawling on it to get the beaver hat it had snagged in the water.

Fogg jabbed an elbow into Fargo's side and pointed to the riffle. A man's body had washed onto the sandbar. "Hollister," Fogg muttered.

They moved to the starboard railing, looked aft in time to see a second body be stopped by the sandbar. Fogg said, "Trouble begets trouble. I warned them about using their fists on other people. But they didn't listen. We'll never know who threw the keel-boaters overboard. Nor do I care to know." Fogg headed for the breakfast table, Fargo for the main deck. He had to know.

Buford wasn't on the main deck. Crutch was missing, too. Fargo looked at the stalls. The mules were gone. The moonshine baskets, too.

Then he noticed Homer, staring fearfully at him. Grim-jawed, Fargo strode toward the stable boy.

Homer dropped his broom and without hesitation, ran and jumped in the river.

Fargo spun and ran up the stairs, through the saloon, to the Vermont. This time he didn't look in on Elvira; he jerked the covers off her. And she wasn't there. Pillows, towels, and upper bunk covers were. Fargo sprinted to Gloria's room, knowing what he would find even before he opened her door. She too was gone.

"How?" he wondered aloud, frowning.

9

Fargo stood in Gloria's doorway and stared blankly across the saloon, pondering his own question. Broussard's loud laughter broke the fixation. He focused on her and Bennett, then shifted his gaze to the captain's table. Fogg sat in his usual seat, the Jances in theirs. The Farnsworths were preparing to sit. Socrates stood behind Fogg. Fargo caught Socrates staring at him much the same as his nephew did just before he ran and jumped overboard.

Suddenly it all came to him. His eyes locked onto the waiter's. Grim-jawed, Fargo strode toward Socrates.

The waiter backed across the foyer to a closed stateroom door. His eyes darted left and right. Fargo saw beads of perspiration form on the black man's forehead.

The forward section of the saloon was gripped in silence. The people watched the big man stalk his nervous quarry. Fargo saw Socrates reach behind and use a key to unlock the door. The waiter spun and ran inside the stateroom.

Four long strides put Fargo at the door. He kicked it open. Socrates unlocked the outer door, glanced over his shoulder, and screamed.

Fargo cleared the outer door just as Socrates dived over the starboard railing and plummeted into the Mississippi. Fargo stepped to the railing, watching as the frantic waiter bobbed to the surface, then started swimming to the far bank. Fargo knew the scared waiter would never reach the shore. He turned and went to the captain's table. On the way he saw the chief clerk had seated himself beside Bennett and Broussard at the adjoining table.

Fargo stood between the two tables to explain, "Captain Fogg, two women were taken by the culprits during the fog."

"Two?" gasped Madame Broussard.

"Elvira Blassingame and Gloria LeBeaux," Fargo answered.

"You said culprits, Mr. Fargo," Fogg said as he returned his attention to the big man.

"Yes," Fargo began. "The stable boy, Socrates, Crutch, and . . ." Fargo glanced at Madame Broussard, then added, "Jack Buford."

The hefty woman shot to her feet and challenged, "No! Never. Buford wouldn't dare. You're mistaken about him."

"Could be, ma'am, but I think not," Fargo replied dryly. "Jack and Crutch are missing also." He looked at Post. "Did you let Jack and Crutch leave the boat?"

Post stammered, "Eh, uh, no—I mean, yes. Buford went ashore to help the men gather firewood. At least that's what he said."

"Did he come back with them?" Fargo tested, for he knew Buford had not.

Post thought for a moment. "Now that you ask, no. Or I didn't see him if he did."

"You surely wouldn't have missed seeing Crutch and his three mules."

Post nodded.

Fargo continued, "That means Crutch left before either you or I arrived at the landing platform. He went ashore with the mud clerk's men."

Fogg turned and shouted to Rafer, "Go up to Texas. Tell Mr. Stinson I want to see him." In a lower tone, he told Fargo to go on.

"The jugs we saw floating downstream were from Crutch's big baskets. He had to make room for the two females. And a cripple needing a crutch to walk

138

on couldn't do the job alone. Homer, Socrates, and Buford were his confederates."

"No, not Jack," Madame Broussard wailed. "Jack wouldn't do that to me."

Fargo ignored her outburst. His gaze fixed on Bennett. "At first, I suspected you, Mr. Bennett. However, you had nothing to do with it. I saw you and Buford talking on the main deck. Want to tell me what about?"

Bennett's face turned beet-red. He lowered his eyes and answered sheepishly, "Jack and I talked about all the loud commotion."

"You can do better than that, Mr. Bennett," Fargo persisted.

"Well, he, uh, did mention, er, uh, Miss LeBeaux."

"Oh? Go on, Mr. Bennett. Spit it out. Confession is good for the soul."

"Jack, he, uh . . . Damn you, Fargo, I don't want to get the man or her in trouble. Gloria is from the Deep South. Jack slept with her in Cairo. She told me so."

Broussard screamed, "I warned him the bitch would tell."

And that explained that. Fargo moved on. "Socrates had a master key that opens all doors to the staterooms. He told Crutch the names and staterooms occupied by single, attractive females. Crutch made all the decisions. Socrates entered through the outer door, knocked out the victim, then lowered her body over the railing to Crutch and Homer, who helped him get her inside a basket. Normally, Crutch got off at Memphis. Nobody would suspect a cripple."

Rafer returned with the upset mud clerk. "Rafer said you wanted me, Cap'n. I got enough firewood to last us until Memphis," Stinson allowed defensively.

Fargo asked him, "Did Crutch and his mules go ashore with your crew?"

"Yeah. He said he might as well get off here and take a shortcut home."

"Did he say where home was?" Fargo probed.

The mud clerk shook his head.

"Captain, do you know where he lives?" Fargo asked. "Does anyone know where he lives?"

Everyone sitting at the two tables shook their head.

Fogg volunteered, "He got off on the west bank, so it must be on that side of the river."

Fargo then asked, "Where, exactly, did the *Gypsy Queen* pull ashore during the fog?"

"At old man Sawtell's cotton plantation, twenty miles downstream of Osceola," Stinson replied. "I know because there's plenty of firewood at that spot."

Fargo turned to Fogg. "Have the pilot put me ashore on the west bank. I'm going after the cripple."

Fogg said, "Mr. Post, you heard the man. Go tell Cy." Fogg took a bite of ham.

Fargo went to the Vermont and got his Sharps, then down to the stalls and made the Ovaro ready for the trail.

Half an hour later he led the pinto and Appaloosa down the landing platform. Mounting up, he waved good-bye to Fogg, who was standing outside the pilot-house. Fargo shouted to him, "See you in Memphis after you get back from New Orleans." He wheeled the Ovaro and rode to the west bank.

The evening sun hung ten degrees over the green horizon when he spotted Jack Buford walking downstream among timber. The Trailsman was on him before Jack realized it. Sitting easy in his saddle, Fargo confronted him. "I see Crutch and you parted company. Where has he taken them?"

"Taken them? Hell, he helped me knock 'em out and throw 'em overboard. Me and him murdered the loudmouthed bastards. They were driving everybody crazy."

Fargo's brow furrowed. "You mean the keel-boaters?"

"Certainly."

It was obvious Buford wasn't aware of Crutch's subsequent actions. Jack Buford had murdered three men. Now he was fleeing. "Where are you going, Jack?"

"To Memphis. Then I'll work my way to Nashville, back to Miss Honey's place. You are gonna let me go?"

"Yeah, I won't stop you."

"Are you gonna sic the law on me?"

"No. But if I'm asked, I'll have to tell what I know. Get along now. I'm too busy to jaw with you."

Fargo rode away.

At sunset he found where the mud clerk's crew had come ashore, and the three mules' unshod hoof prints. He followed them a short distance to see which direction Crutch had gone. The hoof prints headed due west. Fargo feared losing sight of them in the dark. The moon was in its new phase, so he couldn't count on it to show the way. Besides, he didn't know the territory. He reckoned he would wait until dawn to start tracking Crutch. The mules would slow the moonshiner's progress. Fargo dismounted, hobbled the appaloosa, and set the two stallions to graze. He built a small fire, spread his bedroll next to it, and lay down to sleep. He drifted into sleep, looking at the stars and constellations so familiar to him.

The Trailsman was back home, in his natural environment, albeit so far from the forests and mountains and streams he knew so well. Sleep came easy.

His inner clock awakened him at first light. He added twigs to the embers of his fire, put the coffeepot on to boil, then walked to the river to wash up.

When there was enough light for him to track Crutch, Fargo saddled up. The hoof prints in the soft soil made it easy for him. After following them due west for two hours, they angled west-northwest. Crutch was drifting slowly to the north, Fargo decided. Before him the terrain changed to wooded hills. He set the Ovaro and trailing appaloosa to a lope.

At midday he found where Crutch had halted among the pine and made a fire. The embers still glowed. The Trailsman dismounted, dropped to his hands and knees, and searched for signs in the topsoil. He found what he was looking for: two pairs of bare footprints and one pair of shoe prints, but no holes left by a crutch. On closer inspection he saw evidence of a struggle. Bare toes had dug into the soil. Behind them were toeprints made by Crutch's shoes.

Fargo returned to the saddle. He knew he was close behind Crutch, damn close. He didn't want the moonshiner to see him, so he followed in the tracks for about an hour, then cut left and rode about an eighth of a mile before turning to the right to ride parallel to Crutch.

Shortly before sunset he heard Crutch's voice holler at one of the jennies, "Settle down back there, Betsy, afore you buck 'em off."

So they were riding bareback, Fargo mused to himself. Now that he knew where they were, he closed the gap a short distance.

He heard Crutch halt at sundown. Dry tree limbs cracked. Crutch was building a fire. Fargo reckoned the man had halted for the night. He dismounted, hobbled the appaloosa, then crept through the woods until he saw the mules. Hunkering behind a pine, he focused on the women and Crutch. The women sat bound and gagged under a tree. Completely naked, of course.

Crutch, no longer a cripple at all, removed his pants, then shoved Gloria onto her hands and knees. Clear as a bell, Fargo heard him say, "You mine now, li'l darlin'." Settling down behind her round buttocks, he proclaimed, "To do with you what I want."

Crutch had a short fuse. Pumping furiously, it was over for him before it really began. He fell back, laughing. Gloria collapsed onto her belly. Elvira looked frightened.

Crutch finally got over his mirth. He put his pants back on, then tied the women to a tree and rolled up in a blanket next to the fire.

Fargo waited until he heard Crutch snoring, then he crawled quietly to the women. Elvira saw him first. He put a finger to his lips, cautioning her to keep quiet. He was less than ten feet away from Crutch, who lay faceup, snoring like a rip saw. Fargo whispered into their ears, "Think you can suffer a tad longer?"

He watched four eyeballs roll back. The duo nodded dolefully. He pulled down their gags and explained, "I want him to lead me to the others. Elvira will tell you why the first chance she gets. Is he hurting you, Gloria?"

"No," she whispered. "I'm too scared to feel anything."

"Want to say anything before I go?"

Elvira did. "Just so you will know, Fargo, he clamped damp cotton over my mouth and nose. I don't know what it had on it, but it made me go back to sleep."

"Same here," Gloria whispered.

Fargo reckoned the dampness was ether and he said so.

He added, "I'll leave the gags down to give him something to think about when he awakens. Don't scream or holler and maybe he will remove them. Sooner or later he has to, anyhow. I'm leaving now. Sweet dreams." He crawled back among the trees, then stood and walked to the stallions.

For the next seven days, Crutch led around and over wooded hills, never veering from his west-north-west course. In midafternoon on the seventh day Crutch arrived at a tumble-down house having a roofed porch across its front.

Fargo halted at the edge of the tree line to study things.

On the porch sat a woman and man in two rickety rocking chairs. A slob of a woman, she had stringy brown hair, wore a thin dress that hid nothing, and smoked a corncob pipe. The man was frail, looked sickly, and was much older than the obese woman. His beard hung to his waist.

A girl—Fargo guessed her age at ten, certainly no more than twelve—stood beside the woman's rocker. The girl fanned her with a peacock's tail feather. Sitting on the porch in front of the fat woman were several children aged less than ten. And a double-barrel shotgun lay across the fat lady's lap. She and Fargo watched Crutch slide off his mule and step near the porch.

"See you brung some new whores home, Amos," the woman drawled. "Ain't cha got 'nuff already as it is, boy. Where'd you git 'em anyhow?"

"From the *Queen*, Maw." He pulled Elvira and Gloria to the ground and made them stand and face Maw. "Ain't they purdy, Maw?"

Maw snorted, "Guess so, son. But can they bear young'uns?"

"I'm already trying this'n, Maw." He shoved Gloria forward.

Fargo knew he had found the other females. If they weren't in the house, they'd be nearby. Fargo drew his Colt and rode halfway to Crutch's mules before halting. Aiming the Colt at Crutch, he said, "Raise that shotgun, ma'am, and your boy is a dead man."

She laughed.

Fargo heard several hammers cock behind him.

"Drop that toy gun of yours to the ground," Maw warned evenly, all joy gone from her voice, "else my boys will blow your ass to kingdom come."

Fargo dropped the Colt. He twisted in the saddle and counted twelve rifle or shotgun barrels pointing at him. Maw Barlow's boys closely resembled Crutch. All had long beards, ten were barefoot, and all wore seedy clothes.

When Fargo turned to face Maw, two females came around one corner of the house. Both wore torn, filthy dresses and had dirt on their legs. One was sloppy fat, the other getting that way. He reckoned the fat one would be about twenty-two or so, the other not much older than eighteen, if that.

The fat girl spied Fargo and cried, "Well, looky here, now, Nadine, Amos brung me a present this time."

Nadine protested, "Naw, Mae Rene, he's mine. Ain't that so, Amos?"

Mae Rene backhanded her. Nadine tumbled in the dirt, came up fighting. Maw let them scuffle for a while, kicking, biting, clawing, and punching, before bringing it to a halt. "You can take turns on him," Maw pronounced. "Git his gun, Tadpole. You and Jake take him to the pigpen and tie him up. I'll decide what to do with him later on. In the meantime let Nadine and Mae Rene have him. I don't want to hear you girls hurting him. Hear me?"

"Yeah, Maw, we hear," Mae Rene said.

Fargo was pulled from the saddle, then taken at gunpoint to the pigpen.

Tadpole and Jake became confused as to Maw's intentions on where to put Fargo—inside or outside the pen. Tadpole argued she meant tie him up inside, while Jake argued she meant tie him outside to the fence. Fargo hoped Jake would win. Pigs and piglets wallowed in a quagmire inside the sty.

Their heated debate went on and on. Mae Rene and Nadine leaned on the fence, awaiting the outcome. Fargo strained to see through the scrub brush, hopefully to see where Amos and the other Barlow brothers were taking the women.

He spotted them just as Mae Rene backhanded Jake. The brothers pulled the kicking and screaming females into the woods on the far side of the house. Fargo lost sight of them quickly, but he now knew the direction in which to look for the other young women.

Mae Rene spat, "Quit arguin', Jake. Put the purdy man inside an' tie him to the fence with a long rope. Hear me, Jake?"

"Yeah," Nadine agreed. "An' make it snappy. We ain't got all day."

All four of them muscled the big man inside. Nadine and Mae Rene held their brothers' shotguns on Fargo while they bound his wrists and tied the other end of the long frayed rope to the top rail of the fence.

Tadpole checked the rope and bindings for security, then grunted, "That'll hold him. C'mon, Jake, let's go see the new pussy whut Amos stole."

"Yeah," Jake agreed. "I wanna lay down on the big one. She's pretty."

They left Nadine one of the shotguns, then hurried to catch up with their brothers.

The girls immediately got into an argument over who would get him first. Fargo was in one hell of a fix. He didn't see one square inch of dry ground in the pen. But he still had his Arkansas toothpick. Tadpole and Jake had overlooked it. All he needed was an opportunity to get the stiletto. Sooner or later the Barlow girls would leave. Then he would cut the rope. In the meantime it looked like he would have to first cut Mae Rene and her sister.

Mae Rene said, "Lessee how much this purdy feller's got." She removed Fargo's gun belt and draped it over the top rail. Then she loosened his belt buckle and yanked his Levi's to his knees, then his underwear.

Both girls gasped on first sight of his limp manhood. "Shit fire, Nadine, look at that thang, will ya?" Both girls shucked their dresses, flung them outside the pen.

Mae Rene held up Fargo's member with one finger, as though testing for weight. "My Gawd, Nadine, it is heavy. Wanna suck it up for me?"

"Yeah." Nadine handed the shotgun to her. "Keep him covered. I'll suck him up good an' hard for you."

Nadine knelt in the mud and fed Fargo's limber organ into her mouth.

The mere thought of him entering either of these women caused him to remain soft.

Nadine pulled back and looked at him. Frowning, she snapped angrily, "Come on. At least try. You hear me?"

Fargo tried, but it was no use.

Mae Rene backhanded him. "Look at that will ya, Nadine? He's too soft fer fuckin'."

"Mebbe he needs some milk, or something, to get his strength back," Nadine suggested. "Screwing you saps a man."

"Yeah, mebbe you're right 'bout him needing milk. Let's go get some." Mae Rene looked at Fargo. "Be right back, sweetie. Don't go away."

"It will take a bucketful of milk," Fargo encouraged. "Don't hurry."

They left naked and laughing.

When they were out of sight, he withdrew his stiletto, quickly severed the rope, pulled his underwear and Levi's up, grabbed his gun belt, and scaled the fence. He got his wrists free while moving through the ground cover, heading in the direction he'd seen the Barlows take the women.

Fargo heard them before he saw them. Crouching, he crept through the bushes until he spotted them. They were gathered around the moonshine still, watching Jake pump furiously between Gloria's legs. Now Fargo counted not twelve but fourteen Barlow boys. A small army, and all were armed. Looking beyond the still, he saw a large shed. The naked southern belles watched through cell-like bars made from lodgepole pine as Jake romped the tall brunette.

Fargo had found the women. The question became how to set them free, then escape so many guns? Somehow, he had to thin out the Barlows.

Again the Trailsman fell back on all that nature had taught him. Fargo knew that humans, like nature's creatures, were prone to not look up, but to watch their footing. Accordingly, he climbed high in a pine that gave him a clear vision of the still and shed. Resting his back against the tree trunk, he waited for the Barlows to leave.

He didn't have to wait long. He heard Mae Rene and Nadine thrashing through the bushes, yelling for help, that he had escaped. One of the Barlows took Gloria to the shed, shoved her in with the others, locked the cell-like gate, and sat on a box to guard them. The others glanced around, obviously hoping to spot Fargo.

Amos said, "He ain't nowhere 'round here. Fan out an' look fer him. Shoot the son of a bitch on sight. I knowed Maw made a mistake giving him to the girls. Kill the big bastard."

The Barlows scattered in all directions.

Fargo chuckled, for he had dispersed all but the one guarding the women. And he posed no problem to the big man sitting in the tree. The Trailsman waited until the last of the Barlows were out of his sight. If he couldn't see them from his lofty perch, then they couldn't see him. Quietly, he shinnied down the tree. He worked his way behind the shed. Peeking through cracks, he counted nine nicely rounded fannies. He wondered which of the seven he didn't recognize belonged to Regina McRae. He would soon find out.

Stiletto in hand, Fargo moved to the left front corner of the shed. He would give the guard a chance, albeit slight. He cocked his arm to throw, coughed to draw the guard's attention, then stepped around the corner.

The guard sprung to his feet and aimed his shotgun at Fargo, too late to avoid the tumbling blade that buried in his heart. He dropped like a bagful of rotten potatoes.

Fargo removed and cleaned his stiletto, and fished in the man's pockets to find the key to the big lock.

Elvira whispered, "Hurry, Fargo."

He found the key. Inserting it in the lock, he told the females, "Stay quiet and follow me. Which one of you is Regina?"

Regina held up her hand.

Elvira said, "I've already told her why we are here. Hurry, Fargo."

He gently swung the gate open, then relieved the dead guard of the shotgun and all spare shells in his pockets. He motioned the shapely females to proceed, and led them into the woods behind the shed. He'd watched two Barlows go in that direction, so he reckoned he would get them first. Cupping Elvira's left ear, he whispered, "Do you want to help me flush them out in the open? Nod if you do."

Elvira didn't hesitate. She nodded.

Fargo whispered. "Then walk ahead of us. They won't shoot you. Walk humming a tune."

Elvira nodded.

Fargo watched her move through the bushes and start humming. He and the others followed at a safe distance.

Soon, his wild-creature hearing detected one of the Barlows whisper to the other, "Damn, Rufus let 'em git out."

"Catch her," the other voice whispered back. "I'll go see why Rufus let 'em out."

Fargo heard him move through the bushes on his right, headed for the shed.

The other one surprised Elvira. She gasped. "Let go of my arm. You're hurting me."

Fargo parted the bush limbs. The man had Elvira's right arm twisted behind her back. He snarled, "I ain't hurting you none, so don't git sassy with me. You hear?"

Fargo threw the stiletto. It buried hilt-deep between the fellow's shoulder blades. The man groaned his dying breath, sunk to his knees, grabbed Elvira's legs, then slid to the ground, dead before he met it. Fargo handed Elvira the man's rifle, then searched his pockets for extra cartridges. He found four. Handing them to her, he whispered to the others, "Let's get the hell out of here."

He led them atop a hill overlooking the house. He told them to lie flat, then crouched behind a big rock and peered around one end of it to observe the house. Six of the remaining Barlow boys stood behind the house, talking with Mae Rene, Nadine, and Maw Barlow. Fargo couldn't make out their conversation, but Maw was fighting mad. She belted Amos in the mouth, then screamed loud enough for Fargo to hear, "Find him. Kill his ass. He killed two of your kin."

149

Fargo watched them leave. Two headed south, two north, and two east. Fargo hunkered in the west. But that didn't mean he was safe. There were six other Barlows somewhere in the woods.

He crawled back to the women, explained his plan in a low tone of voice. "We wait here till dark or one of them discovers us. If we're not discovered, I'll work my way down to my horse and Elvira's war pony, then come back for you all. Now, I need to know if there is only a dozen of them left, not counting the girls or their parents."

"Yes, that's all of them," Regina answered curtly.

"Not necessarily," an ash-blonde challenged.

"Who are you?" Fargo asked.

"Penelope Suddeth," she answered, and added, "I've been here the longest, since December. These hills are crawling with Barlows. I ought to know. Everyone of them took me before Rebecca got caged up with me. The Barlow clan is huge in numbers."

A sloe-eyed, auburn-haired belle interrupted. "They all came to look at me and Penny. We were made to stand on boxes so they could see better."

"And feel us," Penelope added.

"Then Amos auctioned us off to the highest bidder," Sloe-eyed hastened to say. "Just like slaves."

"I take it you're Rebecca Carlisle?" Fargo asked.

"Yes," Rebecca scanned her sisters' faces. "The clan stood and picked their noses while they watched the highest bidders yank us off the boxes and shove us to our hands and knees."

Fargo crawled back to the rock to wait and watch. The Barlows began returning to the house at sunset. Amos and his partner were the last to emerge from the shadowy tree line. Before entering the house through the back door, Amos pulled the Colt from his rope belt and showed it to the other man. Fargo raised his eyes and scanned the clearing in front of the house. The two stallions nibbled grass near the tree line. He couldn't tell whether or not they had taken his Sharps from its saddle case. His stare moved back to the house. Fargo muttered, "They are all in one place," then thought, I'm not leaving without my guns. It's high time the Barlows got their comeuppance.

He stood and told the girls he was leaving for the house. They watched him walk down the hill and disappear into the heavy shadows.

Fargo stayed in the tree line while he worked his way to the stallions. Smoke wafted out the chimney of the house. Lamplight spilled through the windows and front screen door. He heard the rattle of knives and forks on plates. The Barlows were eating. Good, he thought. Keeping one eye on the screen door, he approached the Ovaro. He saw the Sharps stock protruding from the saddle case.

As he reached for it, the appaloosa whinnied and started pawing the ground. Fargo glanced to see what the problem was. A coiled snake was about to strike at the horse. Backing up, the appaloosas took a strain on the trailing rope.

In that instant the screen door banged open.

Both barrels of a shotgun fired. Buckshot whizzed over Fargo's head, shredding tree leaves behind him.

In one swift movement, he withdrew the Sharps, spun, and fired.

Maw Barlow screamed, dropped the smoking shotgun, and tumbled down the steps.

The Trailsman was armed with firepower he could count on to spit burning bullets. If the Barlow boys inside the house thought he would run into the woods, they had another thought coming. Boldly, he ran toward the front door.

Blasting inside, he opened fire. Five of the dozen Barlow men fell in rapid succession. Fargo made it an even half-dozen when he drew his Arkansas toothpick and buried it in Lem Barlow's stomach.

It all happened so fast that the Barlows didn't know what to do. Confused, Tadpole jerked his triggers. Buckshot tore a tight pattern in the screen door. A rifle fired. The slug hit and exploded a lamp.

Fargo dived across the food-laden table and yanked his Colt from Amos' rope belt.

Mae Rene screamed like a stuck hog and backhanded the air. Nadine fainted.

The coal oil from the shattered lamp left a burning swath. Flames sprouted on the dry wooden floor.

Barlows dived through the windows. Amos and one other fled through the back door.

Mae Rene, terror in her piggy eyes, gasped, "Please, don't shoot me. I'll fuck you real good. You'll see." She dropped to all fours.

Fargo shook his head, then tore the hinges from the screen door when he bolted straight through it. Rifle fire and shotgun blasts chased him to the Ovaro. He leapt into the saddle. He didn't need to dig his heels into the stallion's flanks; the pinto charged into the woods, with the appaloosa following right behind him.

Fargo circled back to the belles. All nine were as nervous as whores in church.

Elvira said, "We thought they had killed you."

"Come, now," he replied smugly. "Twelve or thirteen against a bona fide Trailsman is even odds." He glanced among the girls' upturned faces. "Are you ready to get out of here?" When they quickly nodded, he told Elvira and Gloria to hop astride the appaloosa. "Regina, you ride in front of me. I want to talk to you." He extended a hand for her to take.

Regina rebelled. "You mean you want to feel all over my body. You men are all alike. No. I'll walk."

"Suit yourself, honey."

"I'll ride with you," Penelope offered, and grasped his hand. Hiking the prettiest leg Fargo had seen in a month of Sundays, Fargo yanked her up into the saddle. He set the Ovaro to walk.

Going down the hill, he cut right to skirt the Barlow house, which burned furiously. The Barlow children, the two older girls, and Pa stood out back and watched flames devour their pitiful home. Now and then a gun fired and echoed in the hills. The Barlow

152

boys were hearing boogers behind every tree or bush. Fargo moved away from the gunfire.

After two hours of threading their way through vines and clinging brush, the females grew weary and complained. Fargo hadn't heard a shot during the last hour. But that didn't mean the escape was complete. He encouraged them to press on awhile longer.

The moon rose and with it their pleas to stop for rest. Fargo halted on the bank of a swift-flowing river. The exhausted women dropped onto the cool grass. Fargo dismounted and helped Penelope down.

He cautioned the girls, "Stay still and quiet. One or more of them might still be around."

Fargo didn't spread his bedroll this night. Neither did he sleep anywhere near the women. He leaned against a huge, smooth river rock and drifted into sleep, watching the shapely belles cuddle for warmth.

The loud retort of a .52 Spencer jarred him awake.

The slug caromed off the rock above his head and whined away toward the morning sun.

The Barlows had found them.

10

Reflexes, honed razor-sharp from countless prior attempts on the Trailsman's life, put the Sharps in his hand and caused him to dive forward onto the grass. The Spencer roared a second time. The bullet knocked a chink out of the rock where Fargo's head had been only a split second ago.

Panic-stricken, the screaming women ran helter-skelter into the woods, from where the shots were fired.

Fargo commenced crabbing to this left, where a big, rotted tree trunk lay at the edge of the grass. The Spencer fired again; the slug dug into the grass by his right boot. Fargo glimpsed a Barlow bracing the Spencer on the pine that he stood behind.

He made it to the fallen tree, scooted down its length, raised, and fired. As he suspected, the Barlow was aiming where he last saw the big man. The Sharps bullet tore off half the bearded man's head.

Through the females' screams, Fargo heard more Barlows running through the dense undergrowth, coming toward him. He yelled to the women, "Run and jump in the river. It's our only chance. Hurry!" He whistled to the Ovaro. Ears perked, he rushed to Fargo.

All the women except Elvira ran and dived into the river. Elvira had been in melees before. She knew the value of a horse. She chased the appaloosa to the bank and slapped his rump to make it leap into the water. Fargo did the same with the pinto. Then, together, he and Elvira plunged into the river.

A fusillade of rifle bullets and buckshot peppered all around the swimmers caught in the swift current. Fargo saw six Barlows running along the bank, trying to keep up with him and having a hard time in the attempt. The same ground cover that harassed the naked females during the night flight slowed down the Barlows' progress.

Soon, they were out of Fargo's sight. He glanced about to take a head count. All the belles were stroking to beat hell. Then heard a new sound: crashing water. Up ahead, the river narrowed considerably in a gap formed by two sheer, rocky cliffs that towered high. Churning white water shot through the gap. There was no escaping the white water.

Fargo yelled encouragement. "We will make it!" for all the good it did. The racing water fairly crashed and foamed, drowning out all other sounds.

The women screamed as they were swept into the gap. The last Fargo saw of them, they were tumbling head over bare heels. Then he, too, started the fast ride. The torrent on the other side of the gap hurled him high. Fargo bobbed to the surface only to find he had been thrown into a wide eddy of slow-swirling water. All the women, and the horses too, treaded water nearby. Fargo did not have to tell them to make for the bank.

One by one they clambered ashore and fell exhausted.

A shot rang out.

Penelope screamed.

Fargo rolled onto his back, searched for the rifleman. Another shot rang out.

Gloria LeBeaux grunted.

Fargo spotted the smoking gun barrel atop the rocky wall on the far side of the gap. Amos Barlow knelt and drew a bead on his next victim. Fargo shot him in the chest before he could squeeze off another round. Amos collapsed, rolled off the cliff, and plummeted into the water maelstrom.

Elvira shouted, "Penny and Gloria have been hit."

Fargo calmly scanned the cliffs and far bank for other Barlows. Seeing none, he went to see about the wounded women. Gloria lay dead. Barlow's second shot hit between her shoulder blades. Fargo moved to Penelope, who gasped for breath. Her hand clutched the bloody hole in her abdomen. Fargo knew she was close to death.

Penelope did, too. Her eyes pled as she choked out, "Please don't tell my folks the truth about what happened to me. I'm so ashamed."

"There is nothing for you to be ashamed about," Fargo replied in a soothing tone of voice. "You didn't willingly submit."

Her eyes closed and she relaxed.

Fargo stood and saw the others crying. "We will bury them," he began, "then clear out of here." He picked up a sturdy, dead tree limb and started digging a common grave.

An hour later he lowered the two shapely bodies into the shallow pit and laid them side by side facing each other. Then he covered them with soil and rocks. Rebecca stuck a cross fashioned out of tree limbs at the head of the grave, then offered a prayer.

After the prayer, Elvira and Rebecca got on the appaloosa. Fargo put Frances Anne Budreaux and Velma Thackery on his saddle. Nobody looked back as they started walking away from the river and grave.

Fargo checked the angle of the sun. He wondered aloud, "Any of you know where we are?"

Rebecca turned and looked down at him. "I do. That was the White River. Peavine Barlow told me the house sat just below the Missouri state line. Tucker Hollow in the Ozarks."

Nodding, Fargo dropped back to guard the rear ends, which fairly rolled and swayed.

Eight sunrises later he smelled the mighty Mississippi River. Shortly thereafter they arrived on its west bank. Four towering columns of billowing jet-black smoke rose above treetops on a bend downstream.

Elvira's voice muttered from behind him, "Steamboats. Memphis?"

"We'll soon find out," Fargo answered, and started walking again.

At noon, Memphis came into view. They saw the ferry crossing to the west bank a short distance downstream. He halted the women. "I'll take the ferry, buy you ladies some clothes, then come back and take you into town. Stay out of sight while I'm gone."

They burst out laughing. He turned and walked away, shaking his head.

In town, he found a dress shop. The two older female clerks chorused, "You want dresses for seven women . . . all the same size?"

The thinner of the two added, "And what might that size be?"

Fargo didn't know. He indicated their heights by holding one hand just below his shoulders, then carving their shapely outlines in the air.

"Size ten," the heavier clerk suggested.

The clerks began packing dresses and undergarments into boxes. Fargo told them to throw in shoes also. "What sizes?" the heavier clerk asked.

Without looking, Fargo said, "Yours." He wanted out of there.

He saw there was no way for him to carry all the boxes. The heavier clerk stepped to the front door and called to three straw-hatted boys playing tag in the street. "Hey! You kids want to earn a nickel apiece?"

"A whole nickel?" they chorused. "You bet, Mrs. Selman," the older boy said.

Fargo handed the boxes to the three.

Mrs. Selman stood in the doorway and watched them march to the ferryboat landing.

Crossing the river, the boat crew kept glancing from the ribbon-tied boxes to the big man who brought the items aboard. Fargo explained, "Gifts," and let it go at that.

On the west bank, he had one of the crew load his hands and arms with the stuff. The crew watched him walk away, keeping everything balanced, but shakily so.

Velma was the first to see him coming. She squealed and clapped when she saw the boxes.

Boxes were ripped open, dresses held up, several exchanges were made, then all pulled on undergarments and got into their dresses. The shoes went on last. Several of the women complained that their shoes were too tight. Fargo told them their feet enlarged because of running around barefoot. They left the shoes behind, choosing to walk barefoot instead.

On the way to the ferry boat Fargo told them, "I saw the *Gypsy Queen* moored to the wharf."

"Headed upstream?" Elvira asked.

"Think so," Fargo answered.

"Then we're in luck," she said.

Fargo wondered who all "we" were. Regina obviously intended to head upstream, but the others . . . ?

He was still wondering when they reached the other side. "You ladies will need passage home," he said, and pulled General McRae's expense money out of his hip pocket.

Rebecca, Frances Anne Budreaux, Agatha Marie Deleconte, Velma Thackery, and Marybeth Merriweather opted for passage money. He handed each twenty dollars, then looked at Elvira.

She said, "I've changed my mind about returning to Atlanta. I want to go to Cairo."

"Suit yourself," Fargo offered.

Fargo wondered why in hell she wanted to go to Cairo. He saw nothing at Cairo that appealed to him. But he nodded nonetheless.

He watched five shapely, nice fannies walk away, then led the other two females and two stallions to the *Gypsy Queen*. Mr. Post stood at the main deck end of the gangplank. "How much for two first-class tickets to Cairo," Fargo asked, "and one to St. Louis?"

"Two staterooms?" the chief clerk inquired, glancing at Regina and Elvira.

"No, three," Fargo answered.

Post's eyebrows raised. "Oh, a dollar and a half each to Cairo, two even to St. Louis."

Fargo gave him the money, told the women he would look after the horses, then he would meet them in the saloon.

He found Fogg had hired a mature black man to take care of the horses. Fargo handed him a dollar. "Bathe the stallions. Give them plenty of good oats, fresh straw to lay on."

He went to the saloon. He saw Fogg had replaced Socrates with a much older, less muscular waiter. Rafer and Jeansonne broke huge smiles when they saw Fargo. He stepped to the bar, threw both a grin and a wink, and ordered a shot of bourbon.

While Jeansonne poured, Rafer allowed, "Glad to see you back, Mr. Fargo. Things got sort of dull 'round here after you left."

Between sips from the bourbon, Fargo inquired about Bennett. The man remained an enigma to him.

The expressions on both bartenders took a dramatic change. Jubilance gave way to granitelike seriousness. Rafer answered, "Mr. Bennett got himself killed in New Orleans. Shot dead as a doornail."

"Oh! What over? A woman?"

"No, sir. No woman was involved. Not directly, anyhow, meaning she didn't pull the trigger. Some say she told on him. Some say Mr. Bennett got too close to the truth. Whatever that means. Anyhow, he got shot dead."

Fargo spied Post coming toward him from the starboard staterooms. Post smiled when he joined the big man. "I just wanted to say Cap'n Fogg will be pleased to know you are back. He's in the pilothouse. I'll go inform him of your presence. Miss Blassingame told me some of how you rescued her and the other ladies. Cap'n Fogg will be eager to know all about it." Post handed Fargo the key to the Vermont. "I put Miss Blassingame in the Rhode Island and Miss McRae in the Pennsylvania."

Fargo nodded and watched Post hurry from the

saloon. Rafer and Jeansonne appeared curious. Fargo tossed them a tidbit, knowing that they would learn more from visitors at the bar. "Nothing much to tell. All in a day's work. Well, I better go look in on my womenfolk. See you later."

Walking away, he heard Rafer say, "That man sure does know how to live. Don't he, Jeansonne?"

A loud, long blast on the whistle changed his course. Fargo went out onto the gallery to watch the *Gypsy Queen* pull away from the wharf. He was eager to leave. Soon he would return to nature's civilization. But not before a short stop to divest himself of Regina McRae at Fort Laramie.

Standing at the railing, his thoughts turned to Regina. Thus far she had treated him aloofly, almost ice-cold. He wondered why. Not once had she thanked him for rescuing her, as all the others did. Not that he expected any thanks. Regina had snapped at him when he offered her the chance to ride in his saddle. Most of all she continuously stared at him, stared as though building up a great hatred for him. Well, he thought, I won't have to put up with that nonsense much longer. In the end he decided Regina's bitterness was directed to men in general, not him alone. He quit thinking about Regina, sat, and watched the scenery pass by.

Shortly, Captain Fogg came down from the pilot-house and joined him. The sun was directly overhead when they started talking. It would set before they finished. Fargo told all that had happened, including the loss of Mistresses Suddeth and LeBeaux.

Fogg expanded on the fate of William Bennett. He told Fargo that Bennett had a lover in New Orleans. She told persons from the Deep South everything she learned from Bennett. Fogg reckoned those persons were deeply involved in maintaining a status quo in regard to the slavery issue.

Waiters brought the two men shots of whiskey and bourbon, poured a virtual endless number of cups of coffee before one interrupted to say that dinner was being served. Only then did they rise and move to the dinner table.

Elvira and Regina were already seated at the captain's table. They appeared rested, none the worse for the ordeal. Fargo marveled at their resilience. There they sat calmly feasting on French cuisine, as though they had grown up eating it. Fargo did, however, perceive something was in the wind. Elvira was strangely silent. That wasn't like her.

Fargo ate, then excused himself and went to the Vermont and stretched out on the floor. He drifted asleep not intending to.

Sometime later a gentle rapping on the outer door awakened him. Opening the door, he saw Elvira smiling. "What do you want, Elvira?"

"We want to talk to you. We're in Regina's cabin. She sent me to get you."

Curious, Fargo shut the door. "Lead on, Elvira."

Inside the Pennsylvania, Regina lounged on the bottom bunk. Fargo closed the door and leaned his back to it. Elvira climbed to the upper bunk. Fargo asked, "I'm here. So what do we talk about?"

Crossing her legs at the knees, Elvira finally spoke. "Fargo, we have something to tell you, and you won't like hearing it."

"Try me," he replied dryly.

"We're going to work in Miss Honey's whorehouse in Cave-in Rock."

"Oh?" He glanced at Regina. "You, too?"

"Sure am," Regina answered. "If she wants me. I'm not going back to Laramie with you or anyone else. I hated being an army brat, and I hated it even more after I grew up. My father is a disciplinarian. He regimented me and my mother. She died an early death from both. Well, I'm not going to. Tell him anything you like, but I'm not going back with you."

Regina seemed to have made up her mind. He didn't want to argue with her, so he simply nodded.

Elvira explained, "Gloria and I met Miss Honey in the ladies' cabin. She already knew Jack Buford had bedded Gloria. So, when Gloria asked if she could go to work for her, Miss Honey offered her a job at Cave-in Rock. Then she turned to me and made me the same offer. I'd never thought about making a living flat on my back. Now, I did. I told myself it sure beat hell out of being a starving preacher's wife. And that would be how it would end up. So, I accepted Miss Honey's offer. I planned to tell you in Memphis."

Fargo knew why he had been invited. He removed his hat and neckerchief first. The question was, which female would he wrestle with first?

As two pairs of hands helped him complete undressing, Fargo realized that this was one question that required no answer.

bedded Carrie. So, when Gloria asked if she could go
to work for her, Miss Honey offered her a job at
she asked

LOOKING FORWARD!

**The following is the opening
section from the next novel in the exciting
Trailsman series from Signet:**

THE TRAILSMAN #114
THE TAMARIND TRAIL

*Florida, 1860, just east of the
Ocala Forest where lush beauty was a trap
and death waited for the unwary.*

The big man with the lake-blue eyes swore silently as
he peered across the saloon without putting down the
piece of roast chicken he was enjoying. Trouble, he
knew, could come at expected times and in all kinds
of shapes and ways. This time, trouble came with
short brown hair and a smudged face that was nonetheless perkily pretty. The small, wiry figure had high,
round breasts,. which even the loose tan shirt couldn't
conceal; she wore jeans and boots and a holster at her
hip. He had seen her as she entered the saloon, a
pugnacious scruffiness to her. She walked to where six
men were playing poker at one of the large round
tables.

He had started to return to his meal when her voice
cut through the low murmur of the saloon.

"Goddamn you, Max Garson, what'd you do with
Una?" she barked.

The big man saw her plant her feet as though she

were a gunfighter. The saloon instantly fell silent and the bartender began to back away from the front of the bar. The six poker players had turned in their chairs to look at her, all except the one who faced her directly.

A big man, at least two hundred pounds, with a heavy-featured face, thick lips, a wide, flattened nose, beetling black eyebrows, and unruly black hair, he spoke in a deep, growling voice. "Who are you, girlie?"

"Annie Dowd. I'm Una's cousin and I want to know what you did with her," the girl said.

"I don't know anything about your damn cousin."

"Liar, stinking rotten liar," the girl shot back. "I know what you are Garson. You're a kidnapping, woman-stealing, stinking, rotten slave-trading bastard."

Skye Fargo put down his piece of chicken after one more bite as the man's eyes grew narrow. "You've a real nasty little mouth, girlie," Max Garson said as he pushed to his feet.

"Draw on me, Garson. Come on, I dare you," the scruffy little figure threw at him. "I can put an end to you right here and now. Go on, draw."

Fargo frowned. She was plainly furious, and anger was making her either damn confident or damn dumb. It was probably the latter, he decided. But Garson didn't draw, he noticed. The man had been challenged and he'd every right, but he didn't move his gun arm. Instead, an oily smile turned his thick lips. "You must be kidding," he said.

"Try me, damn you, Garson. Try me," Annie Dowd flung back. "You're a damn coward, too."

Fargo saw the man's heavy-featured face harden. "You need some manners, girlie," he growled, and Fargo's peripheral vision caught the figure move away from the bar. The man moved silently in a half-circle to come up behind the girl, a lean, lanky figure with a mean-looking mouth and small black eyes, clothed in black Levi's and a black shirt. Annie Dowd's attention was concentrated on Garson, and she neither saw nor felt the man come up behind her until her arms were pinned to her sides from behind. She tried to twist away, but the lanky figure had her pinned tightly, his arms wrapped entirely around her.

"Goddamn, let go of me, you bastard," Annie Dowd spit out. She tried to free herself and failed again as the black-clothed figure pulled her up straight.

"Get her gun," Max Garson ordered, and one of the other poker players stepped forward and lifted the six-gun from the girl's holster, a .44 Allen & Wheelock army six-shot single-action piece. Garson's oily smile touched his thick lips again as his eyes bored into Annie Dowd. "Now we'll be taking you into the back and see how big your mouth really is," he said while the others around him sniggered.

Fargo let a deep sigh escape him as he rose and in two long strides crossed to behind the lanky figure holding the girl, the end of the big Colt pressed against the back of the man's neck. "Let her go and nobody gets hurt," he said, and felt the man stiffen.

The man hesitated and Fargo let him hear the click of the Colt's hammer being drawn back. The man released his grip on Annie Dowd and she tore away instantly as Fargo stepped back and holstered the Colt.

The man turned to stare at him, ice in his small eyes. "Who the hell are you, mister?" Fargo heard Max Garson growl.

"Nobody," Fargo said.

"Then you ought to mind your own business."

"I'd like to do that. I'd like to finish my meal," Fargo said pleasantly. "So give the little lady her gun back and let her go her way."

"You just finished your meal, buster. Get the hell out of here or Jack's goin' to carve you into little pieces," Garson said.

Fargo glanced at the lanky man and saw him draw a long-bladed dagger from inside his shirt. Fargo's eyes flicked to the table and saw that Garson and two of the others had their guns drawn and leveled at him.

Annie Dowd, concern in her eyes, had backed a few paces away. "I'll go. I don't want anybody hurt on my account," she said.

"You're not going anywhere, you little bitch," Garson snapped. "And your friend's goin' to learn about butting into other people's business."

"He's not my friend. I never saw him before. Leave him out of this," Annie said.

Fargo smiled inwardly. She had a sense of justice. She was trying to get him off the hook. But Garson wasn't about to let it turn that way. He felt he had the upper hand and he'd use it. But he'd not expect boldness, none of them would. He smiled as he spoke.

"You stupid son of a bitch with the knife, I'm waiting for you," Fargo said, and the lanky man's small eyes widened. He threw a glance at Garson.

"Cut his damn head off, Jack," Garson said, and the lanky figure moved quickly, on the balls of his feet, as he came toward the big man.

Fargo backed, circled, his eyes on the man's hands. The lean body would be quick, he knew, but he'd favor fast slashing motions. That was in his body movements and the way he held the long-handled dagger. His first lunging slash was a slicing blow delivered sidearm. Fargo leaned backward and let the knife blade almost swipe his stomach. He countered with a left hook he knew would appear feeble and then circled again.

The man whirled, slashed again, and once more Fargo let the blow almost land. Garson and the other two men still had their guns leveled at him. If he tried to draw, they'd open fire, so he kept his hand away from the holster as the lean figure came in with another blow, a straight-armed slash this time that grazed Fargo's shoulder.

The Trailsman dropped into a crouch, weaved, and with a grin his opponent lashed out in a long arc with the blade. Fargo ducked one slash, ducked another, and retreated. The man rushed after him, overconfident now, lunging and slashing. Fargo continued to stay in a half-crouch as he ducked to the right and to the left.

Fargo knew he'd not be able to avoid many more of the lunging slashes, the half-crouch allowing him only to twist and duck. It was exactly what he wanted the knife-wielder to think. And he was right: he could only avoid a few more lunges. But he stayed in the crouch, ducking away from a slice of the dagger that tore his shirt open at the shoulder. He sensed the table at his back and the chair alongside it. He twisted away toward it, backed, and came against the chair. He flung his arms out as he appeared to stumble off-balance, a moment of fright on his face.

The man gave a cry of triumph as he leapt in, but Fargo's hand had closed around the leg of the chair as he went backward. He swung it in a short arc and his opponent's legs crashed into it. The man fell forward, his momentum and balance disrupted. It was the split second Fargo had waited for, and he brought his fist down in a thunderous pile-driver blow that landed on the man's wrist.

The knife dropped from his hand as he untangled himself from the chair. Fargo dropped low and scooped the long-bladed dagger up in one hand as the man charged to get his hand on it. Fargo turned the knife up; the long, lanky figure tried to halt his momentum, but he couldn't do it. Fargo saw his mouth fall open as he impaled himself on the blade. He started to fall forward and the long blade slid into his abdomen to the hilt. Fargo pushed himself upward, wrapped one arm around the man, and spun him around to face the others. Fargo's Colt was in his hand as he held the man in front of him, a sagging, lifeless shield.

"Throw your guns down, gents," Fargo said, still holding the lifeless form with one hand. Garson dropped his gun and the other two men followed his example. Fargo flung the long, lean form away from him as his eyes bored into Garson. "He's yours," Fargo said.

"Take Jack outside," Garson said.

Two of the poker players stepped forward, lifted the lifeless form, and carried it from the saloon.

Fargo's eyes had turned the frigid blue of an ice floe as he stared at Garson. "Give the girl her gun back," he said.

"Certainly." Garson nodded and one of the men stepped forward to hand the long-barreled Allen & Wheelock back to Annie. "Seems everyone got a mite too excited," Garson said soothingly.

"Maybe," Fargo said, and his eyes stayed on the heavy-featured man as he spoke to the small, wiry form beside him. "You get on out of here now," he said.

"I want to explain to you, mister," she said.

"I want to finish eating," Fargo said, his voice hardening. "Get out of here."

She hesitated, and a quick glance showed him her smudged face carried concern and uncertainty. But she turned on her heel and strode from the saloon.

Fargo backed to his table, sat down, and placed the Colt beside the plate. "Now I'll be finishing my meal," he said to Garson. "I don't like to be disturbed when I'm eating, especially twice. It makes me very irritable." He leaned back and picked up his piece of chicken and saw Garson motion to his men as he sat down around the poker table again.

Fargo had only three bites of his chicken left and he finished them, downed the last of the bourbon in the shot glass, and sat for a moment with his hand on the Colt, thoughts dancing through his head. It was his first visit to the saloon, his first visit to the town. Snakebird, they called it. Indeed, it was his first visit to the state, and he'd already seen that it was a place far different than any he'd ever been.

Yet some things never changed, he reckoned. Bullies and killers were the same all over. Scenery had little effect on the behavior of men. Or of women. Good was a constant beyond time and place, and evil was evil no matter what the backdrop.

Fargo's eyes went to Garson and the others at the table. They had renewed their card game, but the scruffy little girl had flung scathing accusations. Max Garson wasn't the kind to ignore them. Resumption of the poker game was a deception and Fargo decided to prepare his move first. He rose, paid for the meal, and casually walked past the cardplayers. He felt Garson's eyes following him as he left the saloon.

Outside, the night was warm, the air faintly smelling of flowers and honeysuckle. Each night carried the same sweet smell, he had found. The magnificent Ovaro waited at the hitching post, its jet-black fore and hind-quarters a stark contrast to the pure white of its midsection. Fargo swung onto the horse and rode past two low-roofed buildings. He spied the small alleyway between the next two and backed the horse into the narrow space. The street curved and he could see the saloon. He hadn't waited more than five minutes when he saw the three men hurry from the saloon, climb onto their horses, and go down the street at a fast canter. Garson wasn't one of them, but the three were among his poker-playing cronies.

Fargo moved the Ovaro from the narrow alleyway and, staying back far enough not to be picked up, followed the three riders. As soon as the men left town, they rode along a narrow road that bordered a thick forest of sweetgum, palmetto palm, tupelo, and many other kinds of trees whose names Fargo had yet to discover. Hanging forests, he'd already come to call them, filled with lush flowers and tendrils and vines and always that slightly heavy, sweet smell of tropical blossoms. The horsemen were not following tracks, he noted. They were moving much too fast for that. They knew where the girl was headed and were riding to catch up to her.

Fargo's lips pulled back in a grimace. He wouldn't get involved in anything more than saving her hide. She had a kind of recklessness that came only from honesty, and she probably deserved a helping hand. But she'd have to fight the rest of her battles herself. He'd come here on a job—no final agreement yet, but they'd sent a handsome piece of traveling money. He'd not let himself be sidetracked by anything else, not here in this state they called Florida, a place entirely new to him. He'd told them that in the letter he'd sent back, but they wanted to meet with him anyway. So he had come after finishing breaking trail for a new haulage route into Tennessee.

The road ended as it veered from the forest and became a level expanse of open land. His thoughts broke off. The moonlight let him see the girl riding some hundred yards ahead. He saw the three pursuers pick up speed. She turned in the saddle as she heard the sound of their horses and put her mount into a full gallop in an effort to outrun her pursuers. But her horse was a small mount with short strides and the three men were quickly catching up to her. Fargo saw a cluster of low hawthorns take shape to the right; the girl headed for them. Two shots rang out and she began to veer her horse in one direction, then another as she continued to ride for the hawthorns.

But she was losing ground with each maneuver. The three men were closing ground quickly now. Fargo saw her skid her horse to a halt and bring the horse down to the ground. She flattened herself low behind the horse's thick-chested body and fired off a shot at the nearest rider. It was a trick that worked best against a horde of onrushing pursuers who were going to charge by. But these three separated to circle her and come at her from three different directions.

Fargo reined to a halt, pulled the big Sharps from its saddle case, and lifted the rifle to his shoulder.

He chose the rider who'd circled behind her, drew a bead on the man, followed him for an instant as he charged closer, and fired. The figure toppled from his horse with his arms flung out. The other two reined to a halt in surprise and peered across the open land. Annie Dowd fired and Fargo saw the one to his left fly from his horse. The third one wheeled his horse and raced away. Annie fired another two shots after him, but both missed as he disappeared into the night.

Fargo walked the Ovaro forward as the girl rose and let her horse regain its feet. She had just finished reloading her revolver when he reached her; she looked up at him with surprise and gratefulness showing through her smudged face. "That's one more I owe you," she said.

"I'd say you made Garson real mad at you," Fargo said. "You did call him some rough things."

"He wants to stop me from meeting with someone due in town tomorrow," Annie Dowd said. "I don't think he'll try again tonight."

"I'd guess not," Fargo said as he swung to the ground.

She was a small, wiry figure. The high round breasts under the tan shirt were the only womanly thing about her. For the rest, she gave the appearance of a pugnacious waif.

"Now I can do that explaining to you," she said.

"No," Fargo said abruptly, and she frowned and looked almost hurt.

"My place is a half-mile on. I thought I could explain while we rode," she said, and still looked hurt. "I owe you that much."

"I'm sorry, it's just that I'm here on a job and I'm not about to get involved in anything else. There's no point in my knowing more."

She half-shrugged, the disappointment still in her face. "Whatever you want," she murmured. "You've a name, though."

"No reason to go into that either. Let's just leave it as it is. I'm glad I was able to help tonight," Fargo said.

She met his eyes with her own direct stare. "I am real grateful to you, for back at the saloon and for just now," Annie Dowd said.

"Good enough. I don't expect you'll have any more trouble tonight, but I'll stay the night with you if you want," he offered.

"I'm not that grateful," she snapped, flaring at once.

"Didn't mean that," he smiled. "You're a thorny little package, aren't you?"

"I know men," she said, drawing an air of loftiness around her that didn't fit right.

He studied her with a long glance. "I don't think you know a damn thing about men," he said evenly.

She bristled again. "I know that if you're nice to them, they'll come running with only one thing on their minds," she said, and he laughed. "Well, it's true," she snapped.

"Often enough," he conceded. "Well, you be careful about being nice and being too sure of yourself."

"Meaning what exactly?" She frowned.

"Meaning it may not be healthy to go around challenging people to draw on you."

"You mean Garson? I'd have won," she said. No false bravado, no bragging in her voice, he decided. Overconfidence could be as fatal as bravado.

"Good luck to you, Annie Dowd," he said as he pulled himself onto the Ovaro.

"Thanks again," she said. "I still owe you that explanation. Maybe next time we meet."

"I don't expect there'll be a next time," Fargo said.

"I do," she said flatly. "I'm sure of it."

"Why?"

"I just know. I've a way of feeling things like that," she said.

He waved as he rode away and saw her swing onto her horse. He slowed when he reached the road that led back to town. The young woman's words stayed with him as he rode. He hoped this was one of the times she'd be wrong. She was trouble the first moment he'd seen her, and she was still trouble. The worst kind. The kind that didn't mean any harm. The kind that just dropped problems into your lap without asking anything. The kind that left it up to you to say no to yourself. The worst kind.

Buy them at your local

bookstore or use coupon

on next page for ordering.